A SOLDIER'S TALE

Michael Joseph was born in England in 1914. In 1924 he moved with his family to New Zealand, returning to England twelve years later to take his degree at Oxford. He served in the Royal Artillery and then an Air OP unit during World War II. He returned to New Zealand in 1946 where he became professor of English at Auckland University. He died in 1981.

MIRAGE ENTERTAINMENT
CORPORATION LIMITED
and
ATLANTIC ENTERTAINMENT GROUP
present

A SOLDIER'S TALE

Starring

GABRIEL BYRNE
MARIANNE BASLER

With JUDGE REINHOLD and PAUL WYETT
Executive Producer DON REYNOLDS
Screenplay by
GRANT HINDIN MILLER and LARRY PARR
Based on the novel by M K JOSEPH
Production Designer IVAN MAUSSION
Photography ALUN BOLLINGER
Editing MICHAEL HORTON
Music JOHN CHARLES
Line Producers DOMINQUE ANTOINE and
FINOLA DWYER
Produced and Directed by LARRY PARR

M. K. JOSEPH

A SOLDIER'S TALE

FONTANA/Collins

First published in Great Britain by
William Collins Sons & Co. Ltd 1976
First issued by Fontana Paperbacks 1977
Reprinted 1988

Printed and bound in Great Britain by
William Collins Sons & Co. Ltd, Glasgow

For Mercy has a human heart,
Pity a human face,
And Love, the human form divine,
And Peace, the human dress.

William Blake, *Songs of Innocence*, 'The Divine Image'

Cruelty has a Human Heart,
And Jealousy a Human Face,
Terror the Human Form divine,
And Secrecy the Human Dress.

William Blake, *Songs of Experience*, 'A Divine Image'

In nineteen forty-four I was a bombardier artillery clerk with four years' service, and serving in an Air Observation unit. I don't suppose you'll want to hear the technical details: the main thing was that we spotted for the divisional artillery – twenty-five-pounders, mostly – but also did some forward liaison with infantry, mortars, heavy MGs and so forth. Altogether it wasn't a bad way to do a war, not far enough back to be disgraceful and not far enough forward to be lethal.

We worked with the same mob from Normandy right up to Nijmegen, a crowd of Geordies, very clever gunners and very tough foot-sloggers, but as nice a lot of people as you'd meet in a day's stroll. Then we lost them, because they'd been so cut up and patched with young replacements that they had to be taken out for a good rest.

Now there was one lot, and one particular character,

that I ran into several times. Every so often I'd go up in the jeep with our captain on a forward liaison, which I didn't enjoy very much because, sober or drunk, he drove like a maniac. Well, there was this corporal, and he had the highest regard for gunners because (as you may imagine) a good battery that can put down supporting fire exactly as and when required – close, but just not too close – is regarded as a very good friend by all poor foot-sloggers. And since we spotted for the guns that made us like long-lost brothers and honoured guests. Also he was a Wessex man, from the other end of the country and not quite at home among the Geordies, so he liked a bit of company to talk to sometimes.

In other ways he was a very hard man. He was big and rather clumsy-looking, with big heavy bones and long flat muscles, and he had a big, expressionless, broken-nosed face. Yet he moved with surprising ease and silence, as well as having a gift for stillness. In civvy street he had been a gamekeeper and perhaps a bit of a poacher too, an orphan brought up strictly by his old granny. In the army this made him a natural for the job of sniper or for patrol leader in the shifting no-man's-land between the armies. He was very good at this, taking out small parties nominally led by some young officer, and bringing in small groups of Jerry prisoners for interrogation as required. But he also liked going out for exercise, alone and without orders, working his way as quietly as a big cat along the deep ditches and thick hedgerows of the Normandy *bocage* country, to eliminate some unlucky enemy soldier with one of the well-worn knives of which he would always carry two, one at his belt and one in his legging, or with a wire noose. Or so others told me, for he wasn't given to boasting much. His name was Saul Scourby, and he would have been very bad indeed to have as an enemy, but for us he couldn't do too much. As I waited for my captain to come back from his session at the officer's mess (where he was also well taken care of) there would always be a place for me by the cook-house fire and a mug of tea with rum in it and a big plate of stew or bully or whatever happened to be going.

The last time I saw him was across the river from Nijmegen, in the stormy autumn of 1944 after the failure at Arnhem, when the whole Allied drive bogged down for the winter. It was a cold, damp, low-lying place behind the polders, with the violent, brown Rhine pouring past on the other side, quite capable of rising and flooding in the dark wintertime. By the time that actually happened we were both far away, I snowed-in in the Ardennes, he Lord knows where.

The HQ Company had their cook-house in one of those big Dutch barns, well blacked-out with tarpaulins. My captain was having a long session with friends in the mess – I think he knew then that we'd be moving soon – and so we sat on as the night gathered outside with its searchlights. The main cookers were off, and the cooks and the fatigue men were playing a grumbling game of pontoon round the only lantern. There was a Primus going to keep the tea hot for the guard, so Saul Scourby and I sat beside it. When he got to telling me about this French girl he'd known in Normandy it was just for something to talk about, for no particular reason, just to pass the time. But it took possession of my mind in a strange way, and I've thought about it so often that now, nearly thirty years later, it's hard to separate what he told me from what I imagined out of it, what I divined, what I added of my own.

I've tried to tell it as he told it, though I know how difficult this is – you can't try to reproduce an English lower-class accent without seeming to patronize it. Look at Kipling, for example, though he gets away with it because he loved people and because time (as Auden says) pardons those who write well. One thing I've done is to patch in various pieces here and there, like the woman's bits of stories recalling the France of the Third Republic, which I'd known and he hadn't; but in the main I've tried to write the book he might have written, if he could. Only he couldn't, not because he was stupid or illiterate – for example, he knew his Bible better than most of us, which his granny used to read to him when he was a kid – but because he was a modest man, too modest to be a writer.

So, although it's not strictly realistic, you must try to imagine him telling this story, squatting on a ration-box, staring with his cold eyes over the rim of his mug into the thin, blue flame, seeing in it the pictures he was describing to me.

Did I tell you, bom (he said), did I tell you about this bit of stuff I had in Normandy? Did I? Shall I fill your mug up? Right. Well, she was a lady, and a tart with it. A regular Jezebel, like Jezebel the wife of Ahab.

It was when we was near this village south of Bayeux. Pulled back in support, we was, and having a bit of a rest. A lot of the local people had gone and what was there stuck pretty close to their cellars, because we wasn't too far from the line. Quiet, it was, except for a battery of mediums not far off, that shook the place up sometimes.

So there was the village one way and the other was a sort of monastery place, and in between we was dug in on some old Jerry positions, pretty cushy, really. There was fields around and a side road and some farmhouses.

So in the evening I says to Charlie, my offsider, I says, Charlie, I says, let's take a butcher's up that road.

What for? he says.

Oh, just for a walk, I says. Maybe there's some loot up there, or even a nice bit of crumpet.

That'd be all right, says Charlie, but he didn't sound as if he meant it. He was rather small and quiet, and I don't think he'd ever had a woman. And anyhow I was only teasing him.

So we walked a piece down a side road and we come over a bit of a hill. The other side there was a dip and a sort of open place and a cottage with a garden. We was looking down on it, pretty much hidden behind a hedge, and we could see one side of the cottage with some vegetables growing and a little shed.

Doesn't look like much, I says, and I was wondering whether to turn it in when the door opened just a crack so that someone could look out. Then it opened wider and out come a girl with long red hair and she stood on the back step looking about and listening for trouble. And well she might because you didn't know who might be around – French or Yanks or us or German stragglers.

When she'd had a good look and decided it was all clear, she came right out. She was carrying a wooden bucket which she took to a sort of iron stand-pump in a corner of the garden and began to pump water into it.

Come on, Charlie, I says, let's see if we can chat her up.

So we walked down the hill very quiet like along the road that was thick with dust and soft underfoot. We could hear the pump going swish-clunk, swish-clunk for a while, then it started again, swish-clunk, swish-clunk, like she was drawing another bucket-ful.

Presently it stopped again just as we come up to a little wicket gate.

Hullo, I says, hullo Mamzelle. Parlay voo onglay?

She was just going back to the house with the bucket, and as she spun round she dropped it and it sprayed water all over the path. Her hand went up to her mouth and she stood there all white in the face under that marvellous red hair – real copper, it was, like copper beeches, like you don't often see.

She was so dumbstruck to find me there behind her – I'd come up very quiet, see? – that when she started to run it was too late. I'd slipped in the gate and up the path and was between her and the cottage.

Then she says, Ingleesh? and it sounded silly because she must have known the uniforms.

Yes, I says, now don't be frightened, I says, because we won't hurt you, comprenay? Not, hurt, you. Just want a drink of water and a bit of a chat.

That seemed to relax her a little, but she was still wild and wary. Charlie come up the path behind me, looking unhappy and lost, and I think that settled her some more because he wasn't really terrifying, was Charlie. Anyhow, she stepped back on to the strip of grass so that I wouldn't be too close as I passed her, but at least she didn't try to run for the cottage.

When I'd drawn another bucket of water, she handed me an old aluminium mug and I dipped it in and drank. The water was cool and sweet, like water is from a good well. She was watching me all the time, still ready to run, and I watched her over the cup.

(And as he told me this he sipped his tea and rum,

staring over the rim of that cup into the thin blue flame of the Primus.)

Big brown eyes she had, with very clear whites, and she stared at me steady-like, turning to face me still as I carried another mugful of water to Charlie.

That's good water, I says. Clean. Sweet.

Yes, it is good, she says. It is from the ground, natural.

I know, I says. I live in the country, like this here.

I live in the city, she says, in Rouen. I come here to keep away from the bombs.

I don't blame you, I says, bombing is bad. And you're safe here now. We won't hurt you. We're your friends.

I know, she says, but men are men. But you are welcome for the water.

I could see she wanted us to go, but then she says, Is it to stay this time? Will the Germans come back?

All the French were like that. They couldn't believe that we was there to stay. They had a sort of feeling, a lot of them, that the Germans couldn't really be beaten. Supermen. Well, we showed 'em, didn't we?

Not on your nelly, I says. We're here to stay. You'll never see them Huns here again.

I picked up the full bucket and carried it over to the step and put it down. Aren't you going to ask us in for a bit? I says.

And I think she was just going to say No. Please, she says. But she's looking over my shoulder and her face has gone white again, dead white. You've heard it said, white as a sheet? Well, that's how she was, really, as white as bed-linen. So I turns quick and brings my sten round to the ready, because although I knows that Charlie's there, I don't like anything happening behind me I don't know about.

All it is is three Frenchmen standing there in a little row by the garden-wicket, staring at us.

They're all right, I says. They're your people.

No, she says in a low voice. I know those men. They are here to kill me.

What for? I says.

They say – they think I am too friendly with Germans, she says.

Well, were you? I says.

She shrugged up her shoulders and two patches of colour come back like flushes into her cheeks. She bit her lip. Then she says, Perhaps I am foolish. I had to live. But they will kill me.

We'll soon see about that, I says. Just watch my rear, Charlie. And I walked back down the path to the wicket and the three Frenchmen standing there. They all had black berets and baggy old clothes, and they wore those red, white and blue Resistance armbands and they carried old Lee Enfield rifles and ammo in bandoliers. A proper Fred Karno's army they looked, standing there.

What, I says, are you doing here?

Now there were three of them, like I said, but they were all different. One was just a kid, with black hair and bright blue eyes. One was big and strong and stupid-looking. And one was thin and grey with stubbly grey hair and a few days' growth of greyish beard and very pale eyes. He looked old and fierce like an old wolf. He was the one that spoke, quite well but with a very strong accent.

Monsieur, he says, we are come to arrest that woman.

Are you police? I says.

We are of the Resistance, he says, proud-like.

What's she done? I says.

Then the kid says something and they all gabbled away very angry till the old one told them to shut up. Then he says, Monsieur le Caporal, we have no quarrel with you, you are our friends and allies. That woman is an enemy to France.

She's French, isn't she? I says.

He makes a noise like an angry dog. She is traitor, he says, collabo, friend of Germans. *Putain.* Sleep with German officers.

The big simple one gives a silly laugh and makes the finger sign. The old one snarls at him again.

She goes with Germans, he says, and she is traitor. Informer. She betrays Resistance men to the Gestapo.

And what will you do, I says, when you've arrested her?

The old man said nothing to me, but the kid must have asked him what the question was, because when the old man told him the kid pointed his rifle and said, Boom boom, and the old man nodded.

I turned and called out to her, You hear what they said about you? Is it true?

She hangs down her head and says something in a low voice.

Speak up, I says, I can't hear you.

Not true, she says.

Then I begin to get an idea. Wait here, I says to them. I'm going to talk to her, and you shan't take her until I tell you.

Then they started all shouting together but I ignored them and walked off up the path.

Charlie is waiting like the patient little bloke he is, and I says to him, I'm sorry, Charlie, I says, but I might just stay on here for a day or two. Would you mind very much waiting a little while and maybe doing a message for me? You don't need to worry about that rubbish, I says, looking at the three of them jabbering away at the gate.

That's all right, Corp, he says – and I think he looked a bit relieved – I'll just hang on here and have a smoke. You take your time and let me know what wants doing.

(Saul told me all this part of the story without any indication of how he thought or guessed or felt. Of course, simple people don't analyse their emotions. At best they give a token indication, like: Proper wild I was; or, I was scared, I can tell you; or, I rather fancied her. But for the most part they retell acts and speeches – I says this, I done this – in a compulsive recall and very often in a historic present tense, as if what memory holds is still happening now. They are not recalling but describing what is still present to them. It was all of this, an experience he had relived a hundred times, in speech and act. The emotions of it were just as real to him, and that was why he couldn't describe them, for we can identify feelings and dissect motives only once they are passed. And then, at that particular time, there was something more. At least, that's how I see it – that he was quite tentative and uncommitted, at that stage. He saw her as an available woman who might find it difficult to refuse him. He also saw her as a victim threatened by the three Resistance avengers, whom he disliked both as clumsy amateurs and as silly foreigners. Mainly it was his hunter's instinct that was aroused, sensing prey and enemies, enjoying his own stealthy vigour, willing to follow a trail alertly, inscrutably, and see where it led.)

Go inside, I says to her, I want to talk to you.

So she goes in the door and inside there is this big kitchen with a black coal-range and a big, old wood-box beside it, and a scrubbed table and china set out on a dresser.

I shut the door and she turns round quick at the end of the room and stands there with her arms across her chest and her hands gripping her shoulders, hunched, angry.

Look, I says, I'm not going to hurt you. You don't have to be afraid.

What do you want? she says, but I thought I'd better not answer that one just yet.

You're in trouble, I says. I can help you if you let me.

How can you help me? she says. What do you want?

Suppose I just walked out, went back to camp? What would you do?

She almost choked on that. They would kill me, she says, when they had finished with me.

It's Friday today, I says. My unit's resting and I don't think they'll move before Monday, maybe later. So long as I'm around, they'll never come near you.

You can stop them, you alone? she says, sarcastic-like.

Yes, I says, them and twenty more like them. Amateurs. Civvies.

I was sitting at the table and taking out a fag. She watched me take it from the packet and tap it and put it in my mouth and light it. She licked her lips.

May I have one of them? she says.

So I passed her the packet and she lit one and her hands were shaking. The first drag she took down very deep, with her eyes shut, and coughed on the smoke as she breathed out. It must have been a long time since she'd had a fag, you could see that. Then she says, No matter how long you stay, they will be waiting. They hate me and they are very patient. They will wait.

Why do they hate you?

She didn't answer that, so I says again, Why do they hate you? What have you done?

You would not understand, she says. You English will never understand. The Boches have been here four years. We had to live with them.

She turned round and stood at the side window, where they could see her.

You had better go, she says, there is no help. The longer you make them wait the more angry they will be. Perhaps if it is done quickly –

If I stay till Monday, I says, that's two and a half days. All sorts of things might happen, they might go away.

So she walked up and down the room in her old, green dress, still hugging her arms across her chest, and I let her alone, because even if she was what they said she was, well, she had her pride, I suppose. Though in the end she didn't have much of a choice, did she? Then, it was funny, she says like making an excuse, There is not much food in the house.

If that's what's worrying you, I says, just leave it to me. You hungry? I says, and she pulled a face and nodded.

So I asked her straight, I says, You'll let me stay then?

She didn't answer but she nodded and turned away.

Then I opened the door and there was old Charlie sitting on the step, having a smoke and reading a comic book that he had picked up from a Yank.

Charlie, my old china, I says, I got some jobs for you, is it all right?

Sure thing, Corp, he says.

I want you to go back to camp, I says, and ask

Corporal Bird in the cook-house for a sackful of spare rations, enough for two till Monday and a bit to spare. Tell him to pick good stuff out of the ration packs, and plenty of it, because he owes me one, he'll know why. Then, I says, get me my toilet gear and a towel out of my pack. And ask Micky Godfrey in the RAP for some french letters. And tell Sergeant Grice I'm doing a solo recce up in them woods we talked about and I'll see him on Monday, but you know how to get me if I'm needed in the meantime. You got all that? I says.

So he ticked off on his fingers, There's the rations, and your gear, and the f-f-french letters – oh, and tell Sergeant Grice.

That's a good boy, I says, and bring all the stuff back here. And look in my big pack and get out the bottle of that Calvados wrapped in the spare shirt. And the packets of fags.

Right ho, Corp, he says, and walks down to the gate. The three Frenchies stood there as if they wouldn't let him pass, so I just held up my sten and waved it at them, and walked down to the gate. They stood back and let him pass.

I stood by the gate watching him up the road, and then I turned and looked at them. I'd given them names now: Wolf-face and the Brat and Big Stupid. Wolf-face and the Brat were grinning at me, but angry-like, showing their bad teeth. Stupid just stared at me as if he couldn't believe, or something.

There's nothing for you here, I says. I'm staying

here for a while, so you'd better go away. Allay-vooz ong, comprennay?

The old man pulls himself up very straight and says, We do not go away, we wait. If you wish this *ordure*, you shall have her. You cannot stay here always. When you go we take her and make the justice. We are soldiers of the Resistance. We do not fear you, Monsieur le Caporal. We wait.

What's she done that's so terrible? I says.

Listen, he says, listen, and he is very angry. She was friend to the Boches, she make love to them. He shrugged. For that, perhaps the women shave her head, to make her shame. But this one, she had friends in the Resistance. She tells a German officer, then the Gestapo – twelve men – my godson –

The old man was very angry and upset and I felt a bit sorry for him. The Brat must have caught on to what he was saying, because he began talking, shouting at me, what sounded like names of people.

– His cousin – friends – my pupils –

You're a schoolmaster? I says to him.

Yes, I am schoolmaster. I teach English, I admire – I admired the English.

Well, I says, I've made up my mind to stay, and that's what I'll do. I don't care what she done. I'm staying here. When I go, you can do what you like with her.

The old man translated this to the Brat, and the kid snarled at me and spat in the dust. But the old man just stared at me for a while, then he says, Very well,

Monsieur le Caporal, real quiet he says it, and turns away. We will wait, he says. And he walks up the road with the ßrat following him.

Then Big Stupid comes to life. Cigarette? he says with a cheeky grin on his big face. So I took out my fags and counted out three, one for each of them, and gave them to him, and off he went after the others.

I watched them go up the hill some way and settle themselves under a big old beech tree, on a bit of a bank by the roadside with a good view down the slope. Big Stupid shared out the fags, and they lit up and sat there, staring at the cottage. I stayed by the gate. Every so often I'd look round to see if she was still there, though she didn't have much chance of running away. Each time I could see her watching me through the kitchen side-window, and what she was thinking about God knows, perhaps whether I'd just walk off and leave her.

(And God knows what you thought, and what you're thinking, Corporal Scourby, I reflected as I listened to him. Did he pity this trapped woman? Did he believe her accusers? I think he was a little sorry for both, as well as very contemptuous. Perhaps at this time he was moved by simple lust and by the thought of using this woman who couldn't refuse him and couldn't escape. And perhaps it was none of these things, but simply a hunter on the trail. In his unreflecting way he followed his instinct. At the moment his highest motive may have been no more than a detached curiosity.)

Well (he went on) presently old Charlie comes back with the stuff, so I took it inside and laid it out on the table and made sure it was all there. Then he went off again, like the good little man he was, but he fixed to look in next day and see if we needed anything.

While she was getting the supper I went for a clean-up. The bog was in the little hut at the end of the garden, and there was this sort of old dairy place at the other side of the house where I could wash. When I went to get a bucket of water from the pump, I could see someone standing under the tree up the hill, but it was too dark to see who it was in the shadow, only I think it was Big Stupid – I noticed that they left a lot of the work to him.

So I had my wash and went back into the kitchen. She made quite a good meal of it, with bullybeef and tinned Russian salad. We drank some of the Calvados out of little glasses and she brought out a bit of that ripe French cheese. Only she didn't like tea and she made some ersatz coffee, you know, acorns roasted and ground up, which tasted terrible.

She'd done herself up and tidied her hair and put on a bit of lipstick, and with that heavy red hair she didn't look half bad. We ate our supper and just talked about things, about what it was like during the war, and the bombing, and the rationing, and how the French felt about the Germans and how the British felt about the

Yanks. But she didn't really talk much about herself, and all the time her eyes never left me.

It was getting dark slowly – you know how it was in Normandy, them long evenings and the twilight. She was cleaning up the table and I was standing by the door having a smoke when we heard the Jerry bombers coming over towards the beaches and we could see the ack-ack coming up from the ships in the bay, a proper Brock's Benefit. Strange it was, too, because it made so little noise, at that distance.

She was standing close to me and I slipped my arm around her. She turned to me and I kissed her, but she didn't seem to rise to it. So I pulled her close and kissed her real hard. Then I turned her and gave her a little shove towards the bedroom.

(When he came to describe what happened between them Saul grew very reticent. Like most working-class people, he was careful with his speech. The newly emancipated words which a bourgeois intellectual or writer or student scatters around like verbal confetti had only a small place in his vocabulary. When he used them, they stood mostly for anger or contempt, not love or sex. And they were used mostly in speaking with men of his own class and age, not outsiders like us, nor women.

And like most working-class men he was modest about his sex life, talking about it in fairly general terms. After all, he seemed to do pretty well at it, and had no need to boast or reassure himself. In part,

I suppose, it's a rather special form of territoriality – the animal is nowhere more at risk, more defenceless, than in the act of love. But it's also a realization that this act, deeply serious to those involved, is an absurdity to onlookers. To watch it, even to describe it, is to impair one's dignity. Voyeurs are people without shame or self-respect. So, in what follows, I've had to guess rather more than elsewhere, following out hints and broken sentences in a way he might hardly have approved. In those simple un-Swedish days, he believed in taking his pleasure in the old way, the woman face up in the dark, the man leading, the woman showing proper enjoyment and appreciation.

So with the noise of bombs and gunfire coming in gusts across the quiet and darkling countryside, they undressed and climbed into the big double bed in the inner room. He hadn't had a girl, he explained, since the night they'd been called back to camp for the move to the concentration areas and the slow journey to the beaches. There was this ATS girl but she hadn't been all that keen. Now he was excited and confident, he'd eaten and drunk well and the Frenchwoman was new and strange.

But it wasn't going right. She lay in his arms quite passively and let him caress her, but without response. Presently he pulled back from her and said to her crossly, You'll have to do better than this, girl, or I'm not staying. I've never taken a girl that wasn't willing for it.

Still without saying anything, she pulled off the sheet and knelt over him and began to kiss and pet him. Suddenly, as he realized where her lips were going (I said that he was strait-laced, like most working men) he sat up and slapped her across the side of the head with a full swing of his open hand, so hard that she tumbled sideways off the bed and landed sprawling on her backside on the floor.

After the swift clap of the blow there was silence and the dying sound of guns. She was sitting up, her face and body pale smudges in the gloom.

Qu'est-ce qui te prend, salaud? she cried out, hurt but dry-eyed, not weeping, and he found for the first time that her fluent English was broken up by strong feeling, whether of love or hate. *Tu me prends pour une putain?* She fought with herself for the words. What you want of me? You want me for a prostitute? I make a good prostitute. I do not love you but I can give you *plaisir*. What you want of me? Everyone want something of me. *On se sert de moi comme pot-de-chambre. Je m'emmerde de tout ça.*

And then she began to sob, sitting on her arse on the bare floor, propping herself with one hand and with the other fumbling at her face to try and brush away the tears. He sat hunched in the middle of the big bed, hugging his knees under the old patchwork quilt and the worn sheet.

You shouldn't of done that, he said, I don't like tarts' tricks. I've never held with tarts.

The angry sobbing went on.

Look, he said, I don't want no tricks, all I want is a bit of loving kindness with it.

I cannot love you, she said, you are just a man who takes me because I cannot run away. You should leave me. Let them take me.

What would they do to you? he asked. They'd give you a bad time, wouldn't they, before they killed you?

With one hand to her mouth, she moaned with fear, and there was a silence, then, Oh what must I do? she said.

He moved across and sat on the edge of the bed, near to her.

First of all, he said, stop crying and come back into bed and forget about those bastards out there. I'm sorry I done that, he said, and I'd like to make it up to you if you let me.

He reached out his hand to her. She held back for a moment, then took his hand and he helped her back into the bed beside him.

Now, he said, be a good girl and I'm going to love you and then we'll sleep. Forget all the rest. We'll talk about it in the morning.

He had big clever hands that could coax a squirrel out of a tree or break the neck of an unwary German sentry, master any dog, set delicate snares for bird or rabbit, turn a rod of beech into an intricately carved walking stick. He began patiently to handle her, holding back his raw need for her until she was ready. Steadily and gently he stroked her long thighs and her breasts which were full and soft in the darkness, and her belly and the silky fur of her crotch. She began to respond to him, kissing and touching him, but timidly, afraid to provoke that strange masculine rage again. He began to want her very much, and when he became demanding and pressed her back on the bed she drew him into her. He took her quickly, more savagely than he had meant to, and she seemed to understand and forgive his need. So great was his pleasure that he gave little thought to her, only she said softly some words he didn't understand.

When they rolled apart, he lay beside her staring up into the dark. He wanted to say something to her but forgot. All he could think of was that it had been a long time since he'd lain in a big soft bed, and even longer since he'd been there with a woman warm beside him. There had been claspings under trees and in dark doorways and on sitting-room sofas, but not for a long time this ease and joy. He felt grateful and reached out to touch her. A wind was coming up outside, moving trees somewhere nearby, bringing a flurry of gunfire that sounded almost lazy, followed by a rattle of rain on the window. His hand touched her belly, the darkness spread out above him and he fell asleep.

Sometime early in the morning he awoke, curled up close to her and with his arm still across her. A small sound and a movement of her body had disturbed him; she sighed heavily in the darkness. The window was a square of faint paleness in the dark.

Far off an early rooster crowed, a country sound. No guns spoke.

In the quietness his earliest memories came back to him. Of the darkness before dawn, and cockcrow, and the sound of his mother sighing in the dark in the little airless bedroom. Of creeping out fearfully in the dark across the eyeless bogey terrors of the blackness and the cold floor. Of standing by the bed at last and reaching out to touch the hot wet cheek. Mum, I love you, Mum. Get back to your bed, you little bastard. And creeping back through the desert of the dark to huddle under his old blanket, waiting for daybreak and all the other bitterness of the world.

His mother was a big-boned, florid, fair woman and his father some nameless soldier from the big camp outside Blandford. He lived with Mum in the back room of the estate cottage, with his granny and grandad. Little and bent, skilled in all kinds of farm-work, ploughman, cowman, hedger, thatcher, his grandad had taught him to use his hands. He was kind and firm with the little boy in a detached way, just as he was with animals. He sometimes suffered from tremendous silent rages which he took out on inanimate objects, working furiously with spade or bill-hook.

Granny was big and florid like her daughter, but in all other ways different, placid where the younger woman was passionate, a chapel-goer and a bible-reader. He had good reason to remember them both for they brought him up when Mum left. To take up a good post in service, so she said, and send money home for him. Soon the memory of her faded, except that he would still wake up at night in the back bedroom, almost believing that he could hear a woman sighing in the dark. He went to the village school where he learnt to read and write and figure. During holidays he rambled about with other boys or went out to take Grandad his snack in the fields. He might sit with him contentedly, in semi-silence. The old man spoke little but enjoyed showing him things – how to plait horsehair into a rabbit-snare, or weave a wattle fence, or carve clothes-pegs. Or how to read the warning cries of birds, or smell rain coming, or take direction by the stars at night.

His mother had faded into a distant and rather pleasant memory when one day, unexpectedly, he came home from school and saw the big yellow car standing in the lane near the cottage. A jolly fat man in bright check tweeds like a checker-board sat at the wheel smoking a big cigar. The boy Saul squinted up at him in the bright sunlight and wrinkled his nose at the cigar smoke. The fat man laughed and winked at him, the cigar poised in the air.

And there was his Mum in the front parlour and she was old. She was wearing a silly short pink dress which, as even he knew, was too tight for her, and a silly little tight hat and her face was baggy and powdered. She flung her arms round him and hugged him in one of her moods of fierce demonstrative affection. He pulled away and stared at her. And wasn't he a boy, so big and strong, and Gran had taken real good care, hadn't she, like her very own, which he was, and wasn't the country good for him, of course it was, town was no good for kids, though of course there was another side to it. Then there were the presents, a box of Britains' tin soldiers, Black Watch in kilts and topees with a piper, and a field-gun that fired caps, and a picture book of Robinson Crusoe, and a tin of Mackintosh's toffee. She dabbed her eyes with a small handkerchief as she told them how she'd found a good man and how they'd marry when he made certain financial arrangements and live in a nice house out in the country, somewhere near Epping perhaps, and then they could be all together there.

She swept him up in her arms again, breathing patchouli, then went out to the car. The fat man winked and saluted with his cigar, while Mum got into the yellow car still dabbing at her eyes. Granny and Saul watched and waved as the car roared down the lane and vanished in clouds of dust. He kept the presents carefully in a box under his bed, but she never came back. Grandad had more of his silent spells of frenzied work and began to drink, just sometimes.

When he was twelve he left school and went to work in the fields, where he began to come into his strength. A few years later Grandad began to grow old and careless, till one day he pitched down off a rick he was building and broke his back. They carried him to the cottage on a hurdle covered with horse blankets, and the doctor came but couldn't do much. The old man lingered on for a few days in his bed, silent as usual. Saul stayed with him a lot, watching the restless movements of the grizzled head on the pillow as he caught the call of a bird, or spied the movement of wings across the small window. His last conscious act was to hand over to Saul, as a treasured heirloom, the clasp-knife with its rough horn handle and its well-honed blade, with which he could so neatly skin rabbits, castrate lambs, put a dying dog out of its misery or carve stray ends of wood into Father Noah and a whole ark-full of animals.

The window was a square of pale early sky, across which drove the dawn patrol of Spitfires with a roar of Merlin engines.

Well, next morning (as he told it) I wakes up pretty smartly when I felt her move out of the bed. I kept my eyes shut but I could feel that she sat there looking at me. When I looked, she had turned away and was sitting on the edge of the bed. She had a lovely skin and the sight of that bare back just about got me going, I can tell you, but I held back, playing it crafty, to wait and see what she would do. I'd laid my sten on the rush-bottomed chair beside the bed where I could find it at once in the dark, like I always do. The sheath-knife – the short one – was handy too but hidden under the edge of the mattress. I always like to keep my tools in good order and ready to hand. I was curious to see if she'd try anything. But all she did, like it might be any woman, was to look down at her body, and to run her fingers through that thick red hair, brushing it away from her face. Then she wraps herself in a dressing-gown – sort of purple Japanesy thing with flowers – and goes out into the kitchen. I could hear the crinkle of paper and the crack of sticks as she laid the fire in the kitchen range.

Then I got up quietly and dressed, just shirt and trousers and plimsoles, and I comes up quietly behind her. I slipped my arms around her and kissed her neck. She tossed her head but didn't seem to mind much. So I showed her the stuff she could use for breakfast, the oatmeal cakes and the tinned bacon and the tea.

Outside it was a bright windy sort of day but with rain about somewhere. There was a path edged with angled bricks, and some rows of cabbages and beans. I wondered who the cottage belonged to because I couldn't imagine her keeping up a garden like that.

Like I said, the crapper was a little shed by the far hedge. I left the door open, but it didn't directly face the cottage. I was happy enough there, easing myself and drawing on the first fag of the day, until I heard her cry out.

I had my pants up right smartly, I can tell you, and was out of there, but I could see it would need careful handling. She was in the doorway and Big Stupid was dragging her out, she was making a fight of it but he had a bruising grip on her arms. The Brat was standing there with a rifle, waiting to hold me off. And there was me with nothing but my short knife, which I always carries. So I began to walk up the path, very steady, keeping a sharp look-out for Wolf-face, but he wasn't there – perhaps he was asleep up on the hill.

As I got closer and closer the Kid was angry like a girl. He waved the gun and glared at me and shouted something about the traitor and justice of the people, while Big Stupid pushed the woman in front of him.

The Kid kept talking and shouting, and she kept struggling with Big Stupid. They didn't know if I was really coming for them, or which one I was going to try and take first. So I was able to edge round the Kid a bit, then I got hold of the rifle and pushed up and out, and took him across my hip and rolled him over so that he fell on the path and hit his knees on the brick edging, which gave him a nasty fall.

Big Stupid flung her back in the doorway and came at me, but I'd carried off the rifle on the backswing – it was still on safe, anyway – and I rammed old Stupid in the midriff with the butt. He turns grey and sits down and I think I done a couple of his ribs. Now I know this wasn't kind, but you don't fight by Marquess of Queensbury rules, not in real fights, only when it's in the boxing-ring, when you want to lengthen it out and make a show of it. It's really kinder to fight dirty, because it gets it over quickly and ends the suffering.

So he turned grey and sat down on the path, and the Kid was nursing his knees. And I says, Arseholes, I says, to the people and their justice. Don't worry, I says, Justice you shall have but it's going to be in my way. Vengeance is mine, says I, I will repay, says the Lord.

Well, they sat there on the ground for a while to nurse themselves and get their breath back. Presently they got up and helped each other off, and I couldn't help feeling sorry for the poor perishers. After all, they weren't like enemy, but what else could I have done?

Inside the cottage, the woman was standing there white and shaky-looking with her red hair all over her face and hanging on with both hands to the back of a chair. Her dressing-gown was pulled about too, so she was half naked. So I straightens it up to make her decent-like and I puts my arm around her and I says, Pull yourself together, girl, I says. There's no harm done you, and there won't be neither. Don't forget, you've got old Saul here to look after you.

She leaned against me until she stopped shaking, and then she lifts her head and says, Thank you, just like that. Thank you. Now I will get your breakfast.

She stood at the stove and crumbled the oatmeal block into a little saucepan of hot water, with powdered milk and sugar.

Your name is Saul? she says. She had a nice voice, soft.

Yes, I says, Saul Scourby.

Saul Scourby, she says, SS. You know what that means, SS, in Germany?

Yuh, I says, Nazis, storm-troopers and all that.

Not alone that, she says, Hitler's janissaries. His

Imperial Guard, but not like that of Napoleon, no. With the black dress uniform and the silver skulls. The 'angels of death', they call them. I knew one, he was a young officer, dark and gentle, so I thought.

She was putting out my porridge on a blue plate, with a drop of condensed milk. There was that far-away look in her eyes, like I began to know when she was remembering something, specially a lover.

I liked him very much. Then one night we were in a café by the river, the Seine, and he told me a story. There was this village in Poland where they were, and a German car – you know, a *kubelwagen*? – a small car it blew up and three officers were killed. It was maybe an old land-mine put down during the fighting, but the SS were angry to lose their comrades. So they went to each house in the village and took the oldest son, and they took the priest and the mayor and the schoolteacher, and they killed them with machine-guns in the church and set fire to the church. They took some of the young girls and they went away. And it was terrible because he made it sound so ordinary, like a summer holiday.

Did you still go with him after that? I says. And she says nothing. So again I says, Did you?

You know, she says, I had not much choice, but I did not love him any more.

You French lot disgust me, I says.

You do not know, she says, you should be glad you do not know.

Know what? I says.

The defeat, the Occupation. And again she has this sad, far-away look. I will cook your bacon, she says, and she opens the tin and begins to unwrap the strips of bacon from the grease-paper and lay it in an iron skillet with some onions and herbs.

She had an old radio on the dresser, so I turned it on and the power had come on, and I found the BBC news . . .

(He didn't say what was on the news, just as he matter-of-factly left out most of the background detail of the landings and the build-up. After all, we both knew all that. But it gave his story, as he told it, a curiously timeless and elemental feeling, as if it took place within a bubble of space and time insulated from the outer world and all its stir and bustle of large events. At the same time, when you thought about it, it made it all look so small and distant – all that rage, all that love, half-a-dozen people against that huge sky roaring with planes, that vast bay full of ships, that green summer countryside shaking with tanks and gunfire.

If we improvised, we might say that it was one of those background-to-the-news talks, and a bland, confident voice saying, '. . . and with surprising ease normality is returning to the liberated areas, even within a short distance of our front line. Shops are open and civil authority continues to function. Of course not all Frenchmen – or women – welcome the liberation. There are the treacherous few, the hated "collabos", who acted as fifth column for the Germans. In most cases they have retreated where they could with their Nazi masters, hoping to lose themselves, or at least to buy whatever time is left before the final defeat. For those who are foolish or unlucky enough to remain, there will be justice but scant sympathy. As one grim-faced Frenchman said to me, "These are not men, monsieur, they are filth. France must be cleansed of them." I doubt if many would disagree with him.')

The breakfast was smelling pretty good and I enjoyed watching her cook, because she went about it so neat, feeding the stove with a bit of wood from the big woodbox, closing the damper, then moving the skillet and keeping the kettle singing at the side ready to make my tea. It always makes me feel good to watch a woman cooking me a meal, especially breakfast. I told her that and she laughed, but she didn't sound comfortable.

So you are not married? she says.

No, I says, I ain't got round to it. What about you?

No, she says, short-like.

You ain't told me your name, I says.

You didn't ask, she says. Don't you care with whom you sleep?

What's your name? I says.

Isabelle, she says, Isabelle Pradier. Friends call me 'Belle'.

'Belle', I says, that means beautiful, don't it?

So she shrugs again, and I says, You are beautiful, aren't you?

Would you care? she says. A man like you, you want a woman in bed, does it matter, the name or the face? And all the time there's this sort of anger in her against me, but it's all a sort of game too.

I grins at her and says, Well, you know what they say where I come from, that a man doesn't look at what's on the mantelpiece when he's poking the fire.

She half smiles at this, and she turns out the bacon and onions on to a blue plate and puts it on the table in front of me. As she leans over, her dressing-gown gapes open and she looks so good that I reach up as if to touch her. She swings away real sudden, pulling her clothes around her, and she turns away and she says, Eat your food, pig.

So I went on eating and presently I says, You French certainly know how to cook. It was true too, it was a real marvel what she could do with army rations.

Thank you, she says. Perhaps it is because our men are selfish pigs. They should all marry their cooks.

That's not what I heard, I says. Frenchmen are supposed to be great lovers, aren't they? You know – Come wiz me to ze Kasbah, my darleeng. (His imitation of Charles Boyer was very bad, but it must have made her laugh.)

Boyer never said that, she says, and the French film is *Pépé le Moko* with Jean Gabin, it is much better. And that is all fairy-tales. A Frenchman expects to marry a rich wife and then have her for a servant, to be a good *ménagère*, a housekeeper.

Not in bed? I says.

That too, she says, like a servant, to obey.

I was drinking my tea, and I lit a fag and passed her one. Is that why you took up with the Boches? I says.

Ah that, she says. I told you that you cannot know what it is like, defeat. Not just this time only, but the first time, and before that.

I thought we won the First World War, I says.

Look, she says, I grew up with the men who won that war, men who felt beaten and just wanted to be safe. My grandfather, my father's father, was a young soldier in the Prussian war. He was wounded and taken prisoner at Sedan. My father, he was an officer at Verdun, he was buried when the trench was shelled and almost died. Later his men mutinied, he lost both his brothers. La Ligne Maginot, you know, the Maginot Line? It was built by beaten men. We hid behind it because we were afraid. We were beaten twenty years before this war started. All my childhood it was like that, shame, anger, fear. When the Germans came in nineteen forty they were so young and confident. They were like new people, a new world.

Now while she was talking like this she sort of perked up, the colour came into her cheeks and her eyes sparkled. I wanted her to go on talking, because I thought if she talked it out she might come round to my way of thinking. But I was curious too – I wanted to understand how she done it, whatever she done, and what it must be like to be taken over by an enemy like the Germans. Oh, I'd read about it in the papers of course, but that's not the same, is it? I mean, you don't believe a lot of the things you read in the papers, they just make up a lot of it to suit themselves.

(I'd noticed this before, the working-class scepticism and contempt towards what we now call the media. It's a mixture of peasant tribalism with the peasant's caution over his personal concerns, a general feeling that the urban world is a fairground where all the shills and barkers and pitchmen are out to get him, but he's too clever for them.)

There was Jerry fighters about somewhere, because you could hear the ack-ack, which was all pretty rare in daylight. She went on smoking and looking towards the window.

You see, she says, they are not beaten yet.

Tell me, I says again, what it was like. I really would like to know.

She stubs out her fag, then she asks me for another, but doesn't seem to enjoy it. She took the dirty dishes over to the sink and poured hot water over them from the kettle and began to wash them. I noticed that she did things like that when she wanted time to think, little things. Women do that, I suppose.

Then she says, Well, you know what happened. We

are safe there behind our great fortifications, and suddenly there are Germans in France. My father used to go out at night to talk to old friends in the café, and he came home a little more drunk each night. He would say that it was nineteen fourteen all again and there would be another miracle of the Marne, we should see that, and *Ils ne passeront pas*. Did we not still have Pétain, the great old man of Verdun? And all the time the Germans they were coming and coming, and you British ran away – well, what else do you call it? No one really believed in miracles any more. When the Government left Paris and went to Bordeaux some people took to the roads and tried to escape to the south also. Many of them were family people. Old people like my father stayed and said they would not desert their posts – imagine, poor Papa, an agent for farm machinery, at his 'post'! And young people like me and my friends, we didn't believe in anything much, and secretly, you know, we thought it couldn't be so bad, could it?

All the time she was talking she was washing the blue china and drying it and putting it neatly on the dresser.

There were lots of German aeroplanes about, no others. Then the oil-tanks were on fire, you know – Rouen is a big port on the river, and tankers came into the refinery down the river. For two days it was all dark like a storm, with black smoke from the burning tanks. The shops began to close up and there was a curfew. Papa and I stayed home. We listened to the radio and drank coffee. Poor Papa stopped talking about Verdun, he did not understand anything any more.

We had a big apartment, did I tell you? On the second floor of an old house overlooking the courtyard. Too big really, but we stayed on there after Maman died, because we liked it and it was very cheap then. It was near a *caserne*, a barracks, and when I was a little girl the bugles would wake me early in the morning, so bright and clear. But not any more.

So we drank coffee and listened to the radio and I stared at the courtyard, and there was a lot of smoke.

Then one morning we woke up early and we could hear motors coming in very fast along the main streets. We knew it was the Germans. Later in the morning a truck came along with a *haut-parleur*, you know, a loud-speaker, to tell us in very good French that we should stay at home until order was restored, and we should be quite safe. So we stayed home, and there was no light, and not much food. There were more motors, and soldiers marching too, patrols on foot, and perhaps some shots, it was hard to tell.

Next day there came again the truck with the *haut-parleur* but a different voice, with a German accent, to say that we could leave our houses to buy food and other necessities, and that all shops should open. So I went out with a basket, out of the courtyard and up towards the square. And I heard a music, a band. I ran up to watch, and there were other people there too. There were German soldiers marching, rrruhn-

rrruhn-rrruhn-rrruhn, like toys – you know how they march. They all looked young and clean, in clean uniforms, like new toys out of a box. And there was a band, so bright and loud, it made me think of the bugles in the *caserne* and the music in the Easter fair. You have not seen a German band, they have a man who carries a thing they call a *'schellenbaum'*, like a little metal tree with bells – like we say a *chapeau Chinois* –

(Suddenly, comically, she lifted the corners of her eyes with her fingertips, miming a stage Chinaman.)

I know, I says, we call them 'jingling johnnies', they're old-fashioned, nice –

– Ah, you know, she says. It was all so gay, like good children at a fairground. The people who were watching, some were weeping because of the defeat. But I had stopped from being afraid. I thought, They are just young men, boys even, with clean uniforms and a good band. And I could see some other people beginning to smile, and I was smiling also.

Well, I could see that she wanted a bit of time alone to set things to rights, as any woman would, so I thought I'd take a turn or two around the garden and see what lay on the other sides of the cottage. I carried the old sten in plain sight, for the benefit of them up the hill and anyone else who might be watching. I was just a bit wary that they might call up reinforcements and try something hard, but I didn't really think they would somehow. And I carried my hunting-knife on my belt like I always did, but the thin one – it's a ground-down butcher's knife really – I keep out of sight tucked down in my boot.

(As he described this, he took out the other knife, which he had never done before with me. It had been honed and rubbed down to a curved fang of steel little more than half an inch wide, delicate and deadly, and the light ran along the blade like quicksilver.)

Now what she said about the Jerries set me thinking, because I used to wonder sometimes what would of happened if they'd landed in England. Of course, some people reckon they did – I expect you heard them yarns about all them burnt Jerries being washed up along the south coast. A lot of people believed that because they wanted to, but to me it was just a load of cobblers. There was old Churchill saying We'll fight 'em on the beaches, and you can always take one with you. I reckon we'd have made it tougher for them than the Frenchies did. But they might have done it at that, and then most people would have settled down and made the best of it. And if you saw the old four-by-twos and such getting it rough, well, it'd be no skin off your nose, would it? You know, like saying Wank you Willie I'm waterproof.

(It almost made me angry at the time to hear him say this, because I had a pretty high regard for the old Poms and the way they behaved in the war. But it wasn't all heroic, and I suppose Saul could have been right. Certainly, in their present mood of self-abasement and self-laceration a lot of them would like to believe it. The French have made a film to show what it was really like under the Occupation, and the British, not to be outdone, have made a television programme with people saying, "Yes, we'd have been just as bad, worse, vile. We're horrible all right." And there was that film called It Happened Here. Only of course it didn't, because the British still had their twenty miles of salt water, and their incredulity. If that hadn't saved them – well, you can't blame most people for being just born survivors. If they weren't, we'd never have come out of the Ice Age. 16670 Maximilian Kolbe, priest and martyr, took another man's place in the gas-chamber. He was a saint, a great dead lion. Most of us go on living as best we can, in our shabby, doggy way.)

Round the other side of the cottage was an orchard, about an acre of it, cut off from the outside by thick hedges and a ditch, with thick grass under the apple trees, where the fruit was setting, small and green. It was very warm and close there, shut in. The noises, gunfire and planes, sounded far away, and the bees were loud. He liked it there, it was drowsy and it smelled good, of earth and grass and the promise of fruit, and it reminded him of his grandparents' cottage and high summer. He decided to come back and spend some time there, with her, when he knew how the land lay and felt secure against surprise.

Through a wicket-gate he came out on the other side into another kitchen garden which looked trampled over and neglected, the beds almost stripped. Examining the heavy bootmarks stamped into the dusty soil he saw that some of his own people must have been through it and cleaned out carrots and beans and swedes for their cook-house. Or perhaps Germans before they pulled back.

In the back of the cottage there was a Dutch door. Peering in through the upper half, which stood ajar, he had a vague impression of damp, cool air, a flagged stone floor, a waterbutt.

Here, too, in the kitchen garden the air was still, but oppressive now, and with a different and familiar smell. Sniffing, he looked out over the further hedge on to a field with a small shed in it and a couple of dead cows. One was foully bloated, with its legs sticking up stiffly in the air. A half-hearted attempt had been made to burn the other with petrol, leaving gaunt ruined ribs black and sticking out of a mass of blackened glue. The sky was overcast. Heavy metallic blue flies swarmed and buzzed in the field but did not seem to cross the hedge on the house side, as if observing some curious territorial taboo. The familiar sight and smell did not disgust him but it had spoilt the innocent mood of the orchard, so that he quickened his steps as he came round the north side of the house and back towards the front door.

But before he showed himself he stiffened suddenly, hearing the sound of a man's voice. Silently he took one step beyond the corner, neither cringing nor exposing himself without need. A khaki-clad figure was lounging beside the door.

It was one of them Yanks, Bom, said Saul, you know how we was right flank division and liaised with them Yanks. Well, this was one of them, a corporal, and he stands there in his shirt-sleeves and with his helmet loose on his head and a tommy-gun slung over his shoulder. He looked pretty tough, but I thought that I could take him if I had to, because he was off his guard, yet I'd rather not. All he was doing was chatting to my bit of stuff, slow and easy, with a drawl. He was saying, I don't know who this other guy is, Sugar, but I can take better care of you than he can, and I can show you a better time.

Then he must've got a glimpse of me, so I decided to walk on gently and treat our gallant ally in a quiet and friendly way.

Hi there, he says.

She is standing there, leaning against the jamb of the door. She is wearing a blue-and-white-checked short frock and has her red hair braided around her head, which gives her a sort of innocent country-girl look.

I'm surprised there's Yanks here, I says, I didn't know we was that far back.

I landed at Omaha Beach, he says, I didn't see any Limeys there.

Fair enough, I says. Now what do you want?

Belle went on leaning against the door, watching us

both, weighing us up. He turned back and went on talking to her as if she mattered and I didn't.

I'm with a liaison task force, he says, I get around, good supplies, use of transport. I could be good to you.

I got here first, I says, and I'm taking care of her.

You can decide this for yourself, he says, still looking at her and not at me. It's your house, isn't it? It's your country?

She didn't move, but she says, All right, supposing I do not want either of you?

You kidding? he says. You need someone to look after you, Sugar. This is no place for a nice kid like you, not with some of the types there are around.

I was looking him over carefully. He was big, all right, and sort of meaty, like some Yanks are, but he looked soft underneath to me. His uniform was nice and clean, and under the tan his face had a grey smooth look from being fresh shaved, and he smelt like a whore's bedroom. (Aftershave was almost unknown then and considered pretty pansy by people like Saul.) I thought he might be a gingerbeer, but if that was so why would he be after her?

I didn't like the way it was shaping, and then I looked up the hill and I had an idea. Someone was standing under the beech tree watching the cottage. I knew it was only Big Stupid, but at a quarter of a mile distance he looked pretty impressive.

You're in trouble, mate, I says, you're in dead lumber.

That made him swing round towards me, surprised-like but still grinning.

I'm okay, fella, he says, I can't see no trouble.

There it is, I says, nodding towards Big Stupid. As luck would have it, just at that minute the Brat went up and said something to him, so that it looked more like a regular patrol.

I got some good friends in the Resistance, I says. I do them favours and they keep an eye on me. You start anything and you won't get past that front gate.

He looked at her and then at me, then back at Big Stupid, still quite slow and easy, a big man sizing it all up. Then he made a terrible mistake. He reached into his hip pocket and took out a wallet.

I'll make it worth your while, he says, and takes out a couple of English fivers. I'll buy out your share, he says.

I looked across at her without saying anything. Her colour always came and went quickly, and she'd turned white again, but this time it was rage. She glared at him and said something in French. Then she whirled round into the cottage and banged the door shut.

You've lost, I says, and now I was grinning at him. What d'you take me for, an Oxford Street ponce?

It didn't seem to upset him. He was the unsinkable kind of Yank, you know, who tries it on, and no hard feelings if it doesn't work, he was so sure of himself.

There'll be another time, he says. You'll be moving up Monday or Tuesday, won't you? It's all moving up, but I can get back any time I want.

And I thought of what I'd said to the old Frenchie, and I says to him like I done before, When I'm gone you can do what you like with her. For nothing, I says.

Okay, fella, he says, tell the lady I'll be back, if I got nothing better to do.

So I stood and watched him stroll off down the road. You know what they say about Yankee marching orders – Rifle on the shoulder put and down the road amble? Sort of comfortable, not soldierly. Then I went back into the kitchen where she was sitting.

She was sitting there with her elbows on the table and her fists pressed hard against her eyes. I walked up to her softly and took her wrists in my hands and pulled them gently away. She let me do it and looked up at me, still white and sullen and hard-eyed. A braid of hair had worked loose and hung down across her forehead.

You see, she says, you make me a *putain*, to be – to be sold, and bought. You should put up a red lamp at the door.

He didn't get you with his money, I says, nor with his threats.

She was very tight with anger and for a couple of minutes she didn't answer. I just stood looking at her, saying nothing, till she says, He does not get me, but you get me. I am like a bone, and you are the big dog that gets the bone.

You remember, I says, there's those other little dogs up the hill. I'm not letting them bite you.

Until when? she says. Monday night or Tuesday. Perhaps the American first, then the *maquisards*. Is that all there is for me?

And she puts her fists up to her eyes again, squeezing them hard, like a kid.

While there's life there's hope, I says. We'll think of something.

I let her sit there for a bit, then I says, Haven't you got friends? I says, Someone you could go to?

No friends, she says, but she was beginning to think about it and it stopped her brooding. Her eyes were red and her face was puffy and pale, she looked almost ugly.

Don't you live here? I says, knowing that she didn't.

No, I live in Rouen, she says. My family used to live here in my grandfather's time. There was an old aunt who died here. Then we used to come here for weekends, holidays – in summertime. Other times we rented it. I had not seen it for years. I came to stay, to avoid the bombing – you know, your people bombed Rouen. It is an old beautiful city.

It was the river-crossing, I expect, the bridges, I says. Anyhow, I don't believe you came here to avoid the bombing, you wouldn't have had time.

Friends helped me, she says.

Friends, I says, what kind of friends?

German, she says. It seemed safer here. Then the invasion – your people were here, and the Germans went back.

I had a sudden idea.

That's what you wanted, wasn't it? I says. Safe here behind our lines, and cut off from anyone who might be coming after you from the direction of Rouen?

She nodded to that. I was safe until yesterday, she says, then I saw them, those three.

Who are they? I says. You better tell me more about them. It might help.

Well, she says, the old man is Monsieur Raoul, Raoul Lemonnier. When he was young he was a poet. Now he is a teacher at the Lycée Corneille. The big one was working there, at the Lycée, what you call a porter, I think, at the gate. And the young one was an older pupil. They were sent from Rouen to find me. I thought I was safe, but of course there were plenty of others, watching.

Now while she was talking, she'd moved over to the window again. It seemed to fascinate her, knowing that they were there up the hill, out to get her, and here she was out of their reach, for a time. She'd stopped brooding, and I'll say that for her, she could bounce back after a shock. I found out that she'd had a few knocks all right, and learnt how to stand them.

Well, there she was by the window when a bell rang somewhere outside, distant, three times, ting ting ting. And again, ting ting ting. And the same a third time. She crossed herself quickly and looked down, like drawn into herself. I don't think she realized I was turned and watching her, and she started when I says to her, What d'you do that for? I says.

It is the 'Angelus', she says. I am saying my 'Hail Marys'.

You mean to say that you still pray, I says, after what you done, and with them waiting for you out there?

I didn't mean it to sound like taking the piss out of her, but that's the way it came out. She took it calmly.

All the more reason, she says. I have not stopped to be a Catholic.

I was brought up to be a Primitive Methodist, I says. My granny brought me up in it, and she was a God-fearing old lady. I still think about it, and I know my Bible.

All this time an idea was growing in my mind, though there was nothing I could do about it till later on.

So then she began to get me some dinner. It was tinned Russian salad and bullybeef again, and if you'd given it to any army cook he'd have chucked it all into a dixie and made a nice brown stew out of it. But she served it up cold, with a bit of lettuce from the garden and a hard-boiled egg and a knob of cheese, and it tasted good. We'd got talking about what it was like in our childhoods, and I explained to her about my gran and grandad and our life in Dorset, because I wanted her to know how the countryside was familiar to me.

I remember my grandmother, she says, she was always in black, a widow, very severe. She was an old peasant-woman always, she was born here in this cottage. Even though she married well, she was always a peasant in the heart.

But the old lady was kind to her, and every Thursday afternoon when they had a half-holiday from school the old lady would take her out to the cinema, which they both enjoyed very much. Such films they saw. There was Emil Jannings as the emperor Nero, and when the army mutinied and all the chariots were driving on Rome to rescue the Christians from the lions, the audience drummed their feet on the floor and shouted, *Plus vite, plus vite*, faster, faster. He was in *Faust* too. And then there was a love-story, very sad. The lovers were parted, and she was dying, and he was dying too, shot by a sniper in the Indo-China war. And as they died one face faded into the other and back again, their identity in death at last.

Afterwards they had tea in the *pâtisserie* in the Rue de l'Horloge, where there was this big old clock with its gold lettering. They had just two cakes each, every week different, for the *pâtissier* designed all kinds of little cakes shaped like cups of coffee with whipped cream, or small baskets full of potatoes, or hams, or mice, or hats, all made of sugar and paste of almonds. But she was a greedy little girl, and sometimes she ate Grandmother's cakes also. They had good times, the old lady and the child, all by themselves. Perhaps she was afraid of her daughter-in-law, Belle's mother, who considered herself rather superior. With her grand-daughter she could be a girl again, enjoying movies and cakes like a child.

She told me about these things and it was quite interesting and it seemed to make her happier. She was even smiling a bit, and those brown eyes of hers were very bright. We ate our lunch at the kitchen table with a blue-and-white-checked cloth to match her dress, all very proper. Afterwards we drank some more of that bad watery ersatz coffee and had a smoke.

While I was finishing my fag, she went over to the sink to put the dishes in.

O la, she says, the drain is blocked again. Everything in France is like that, nothing works any more.

Leave it to me, I says. Got any tools, bits of wire and such?

She showed me a cupboard where there was some old rusty tools and bits of wire and stuff. I went outside and saw where the pipe ran out into an open drain, and I could see that it was blocked up with old grease and all it needed was a good clean. I soon fixed it, and while I was about it I thought I might as well fix one of the window-shutters where the hinge just needed a new pin. I couldn't help thinking how funny it was to be doing things like that, just as if I was at home and meaning things to go on year after year the way they do, when perhaps neither of us would be there by Monday evening.

The weather was still dull, and as I finished the shutter the rain began to come down, not hard but steady, so that it brought out all the smells of the garden. I took my time finishing, so when I went inside I was wet enough. She came up to me and touched my hair and my shirt.

You are wet, she says, take off your shirt, I will dry it.

So I gave her my shirt and undervest and she made me sit down on a stool while she got a towel and began to dry my hair and shoulders. I could feel her close against me and those beautiful charlies of hers against my shoulder-blades. I could see that she was fancying me and I was pretty well fancying her, you can imagine.

(Saul was smiling, embarrassed, as he said this, and his fingers slid gently down his arms, feeling the flat hard muscles, gently remembering what her fingers had done.)

You like me? she says.

I stood up and put my arms around her.

It's still daylight, I says.

She laughs and says, That is a strange thing to say, and she was standing real close. The stool fell over with a crash, so we left it.

Then, would you Adam-and-Eve it, there's a knock on the door, small and polite.

Merde alors, she says, and pulls back from me.

Don't worry, I says, it's only old Charlie.

She looked put out at this and I suppose well she might, the way we was going. But I thought to myself, It's all right girl, it'll keep till later. And honest, I'm not comfortable about it in broad daylight, if you get my meaning.

Then there's another polite little knock at the door.

All right, Charlie, I hollers, though I laid my short knife and the sten handy just in case it wasn't him after all or perhaps he wasn't alone.

But when I unlocked and opened the door there he was, like a good little bloke, standing on the step in his tin hat, with his groundsheet over his shoulders and the rain running off him a fair old treat.

Hullo, Corp, he says, is it all right to come in? 'Cause I was standing there just in my trousers still.

Hullo, Charlie boy, I says, you could of picked a better time, but never mind, come in and have some of this bad coffee.

Thanks all the same, Corp, he says, but I'd sooner have a cuppa tea, if you don't mind.

So I made him a cup of the powdered tea out of the emergency pack, and while he drank it he gave me the odd bits of news, especially how there was a strong rumour that we'd be moving up again on Monday. One of the runners had heard it from the cooks at Div. HQ, and you know how cooks are pretty good at these things, they need to know about moves because of supplies.

(As he told me this, Corporal Scourby nodded his head towards the group of cooks in the corner of the barn, in the shifting half-lights, and the biggest of them, frowning over his cards, the big fat domineering corporal cook with his broad jowly face and his hoarse voice in almost continuous monologue, a double for Long John Silver.)

And speaking of cooks, Charlie brought out his small pack with a few more tins and a chocolate ration, and some rum. There was a rum ration to be issued that evening on account of the rain setting in, and the good little man had been to see Sergeant Grice and begged for a sort of advance on it, nigh on half a bottle. I let him have a good drop in his tea, and he was proper grateful.

Now all this time Belle had been banging about in the bedroom very cross, but pretending to rearrange things, as a woman will. What with that and the news about the move, I thought this might be a good time to try out my little idea.

So I says, Charlie, I says, would you mind staying on here a while and minding the shop? And as he looks a bit nervous at the bedroom door I says, I want to take her ladyship there for a bit of a walk, over the other way, it might do her some good.

All right, Corp, he says, don't you worry about me. You'll have no trouble with them Frenchies, 'cause I said 'hullo' to them as I come over the hill, and I gave them a tin of bully and some extra chocolate I had.

Bless your kind little heart, I says, you'll get your reward in heaven.

It's all right, Corp, he says.

Then I hollers through the door, Belle, I says,

better put a coat on and bring an umbrella if you got one, 'cause we're going for a walk.

There's some more of the banging, then a stop, as if she's waiting for me to answer something she's said. So I rapped on the door pretty sharp, and I says, That's enough o' that. Now are you coming, or do I have to fetch you?

Pretty soon she comes out with a dark coat on and a scarf tied over her red hair. She says hullo to old Charlie, but she'll hardly bring herself to look at him. I'd got my greatcoat and beret on, and my sten over my shoulder. I took her by the arm and steered her out on to the path. There was a sprinkle of rain. She put up a big old peasant woman's umbrella, enough to shelter the both of us.

It wasn't till we were walking down the road that she says, Well, where are you taking me?

You'll see, I says, I've got an idea that might do you a bit of good.

(Now as I'm writing this, I'm suddenly aware of them, and I can see them trudging down the road in the summer rain. The road is sunken between overgrown banks and the tall hedges of the *bocage* country, and overhung by trees. The road has been pounded by heavy army traffic into dust which has powdered and whitened the banks and hedges, but is now being washed back by the rain. And the raindrops, which began by stamping tiny saucers into the beige dust, have now run together to form a crust which will later turn to deep mud. As they walk they look down at their feet, which are breaking the soft crust and depositing streaks of tan mud on his boots, her shoes.

I can see them very clearly, walking down the road like some Saturday afternoon couple, out for a stroll but sullen, having quarrelled. His hand is on her arm, not lightly. A streak of red hair has worked loose and is plastered across her forehead. Her brown eyes are blind with anger and fear. She doesn't understand this man who seems to want her quite crudely, yet can also turn away in apparent indifference. She fears the hooded violence in him, yet it excites her. What she fears much more is the others, the prowling American and perhaps more like him, and the implacable *maquisards* waiting to punish her as soon as she can no longer keep a protector. Whichever way she looks, it is a bitter world.

He is thinking of her with concern, as a poor trapped thing that should be either despatched or released. Now that a Monday move is almost certain, he no longer feels that he can abandon her. A word, an idea has come into his mind. *Sanctuary*.)

He said it to her, Sanctuary, that's what we're after.

The abbey had a double iron gate set in an arch in a long whitewashed wall.

Not here, she said, trying to pull her arm away from his firm grip.

We'll see, he answered, and gave an impatient tug at the long iron bell-rod. A bell clanked surprisingly near, a single ugly note, and a small bent man in a worn black soutane came out of the porter's office.

You speak English, parlay onglay? asked Saul.

The old man shook his head.

Tell him we want to see the gaffer, said Saul, you know, the boss, the chief.

Écoutez, she said, *ce monsieur est un officier anglais. Il veut parler au père supérieur. Conduisez-nous, s'il vous plait.*

The old man nodded, mumbling. He opened the gate with a big old key and led the way across the courtyard in which the cobblestones were polished by rain.

You are a fool to bring me here, she said. They will know who I am, what I did. There is danger here, just like outside.

You don't have to worry about danger while you're with me, he said. And I thought these monasteries were supposed to be sort of holy places? You don't seem to think much of your Church.

Looking round at her, he saw that her face had that pinched look again.

It has been a terrible war, she said. There are no sanctuaries left.

The old man hurried on before them with his scuttling walk, across the cobbled yard, along an open corridor and into a wide inner courtyard. The buildings had severe white walls and steep-pitched slate roofs, the white walls darkened with rain and the slates gleaming with a leaden sheen. There was a chapel with an ornate scrolled front, and another building that might have been a hall of some kind. But the old man turned aside into a short colonnade, and led them into a room that opened off it.

It seemed to be a visitor's parlour, and little used of late. The old man whispered and muttered to himself as he clattered open the window-shutters and scuttled off, leaving the door open. The room was musty, damp and cold. Belle shivered. There were three high-backed chairs covered in faded tapestry; they sat on two of them. A nondescript book bound in black leather lay on a small table. Over an empty fireplace hung a huge old blackened picture of some female saint with dishevelled hair and gleaming eyes fixed ecstatically heavenward.

You see, she said. It is cold, dead. No one should come here.

Perhaps I was wrong, he said guardedly as he looked round the bare seedy room with contempt. I thought it was a chance we might take. I don't know much about your Church really. It's like seeking refuge in the house of Rimmon.

She looked at him angrily, not understanding.

There was a sound of firm sharp steps outside. Instead of the priest-figure that Saul expected a French officer stood for a moment in the doorway silhouetted against the pale daylight, and then entered the room. Surprised, Saul rose to his feet and snapped him up a smart salute, which the officer returned with courtesy. He was dressed in olive-drab uniform and cylindrical blue kepi, a shortish bulky figure. He removed his kepi and sat casually in the third chair, turning towards the light as he did so, and they could see that he was perhaps in his middle forties, with thick short greying hair and a pale square lined face.

Madame, he said, nodding towards Belle. Monsieur le Caporal. Can I 'elp you?

He spoke correct English, like the *maquisard* schoolmaster, but with a heavier accent, as if out of practice.

Excuse me, said Saul, Sir, we was expecting the father superior.

He glanced at Belle to see if he'd got it right, but she shook her head.

I am the father superior 'ere, said the officer, glancing down at his uniform. Since the liberation (he gave it the French pronunciation) I am recalled to the flags.

You'll be a chaplain, I expect, Sir?

The officer smiled and Saul could see how tired his face was.

In my country, unlike yours, priests are not exempt from the conscription. I am a captain of artillery. It is more fitting.

Like I seem to remember, Sir, said Saul, that in olden times your bishops fought like knights but carried maces, because that way they didn't have to shed blood.

The priest-officer raised his hand in a small gesture.

You are a soldier, he said. I suppose that you do not believe it wrong to fight or to shed the blood.

As for that, Sir, I believe that we may smite the un-

65

righteous. But for a priest it seems strange. Christ wasn't a fighting man.

But 'e was a friend of soldiers, the centurion 'e loved for 'is faith and discipline. And saints 'ave been soldiers.

Joan of Arc, said Belle unexpectedly.

Exactly. You are from Rouen, Madame?

He looked across at her sharply.

Yes, she answered in a low voice. When I was a child they took me to see that prison where they kept her before she was taken and burnt. Soldiers did that to her.

The way I heard it, said Saul, it was some of your bishops.

Collaborators, said the priest sharply. Like as today.

The woman flushed.

Collaborators, she said, it is easy to say, father. *Les collabos, ça se dit si facilement, si on ne connait pas les necessités, les terreurs.*

Mais nous sommes tous dans cette galère, ma pauvre fille, said the priest, and turned politely to Saul. There 'as been great – pression?

He turned back to Belle, seeking a word.

Pressure, she said.

– pressure, he went on. Imagine, mon caporal, five years, men 'ad fear for the families, the friends. God forgive weakness. One must live. But it is another thing for some ones who – betray.

He hesitated, glancing around the bleak room and the grey light that leaked in through the window, the defiant ugliness of austerity. Then he raised his tired hooded eyes to her almost shyly, ashamed of what he must say to her.

I know, madame, he said, your name, your family. I know why the strike group is 'ere to seek you.

Look, Sir, said Saul, she's been too friendly with the Germans, she's not denying that. I expect she's not the only one. But those men out there, they're going to kill her. If she's really done something wrong, then put her in gaol, let her be tried.

Who do you think are running the gaols? said Belle bitterly.

Saul went on looking at the priest, trying to reach the compassion that he sensed in him.

What about forgiveness? he asked, nodding towards the dark painting on the wall, the penitent with her lustrous weeping eyes raised to heaven in repentance and joy. What about the woman taken in adultery? And casting the first stone? Sir, he added as an afterthought.

He had spoken quickly, and the priest hesitated, only half understanding.

Belle translated in a low voice: . . . *la femme adultère* . . . *sans péché* . . . *jette la pierre le premier.*

The priest sighed.

If alone it might be so simple, he said. I know who you are, why you are 'ere. The Réseau Alésia.

Belle caught her breath.

There was a cell of the Résistance in Rouen. You betrayed it to your lover in the SS –

Father, please, I swear –

We think we know almost what was said, and when. I am *résistant* myself. We 'ave the reports. And more.

He leaned forward in his uncomfortable chair, hands clasped together, staring at the floor.

One of the dead was from the village, he said. They were strange people, the Boches, very methodic. They sent back the body for the burial. In a sealed coffin, naturally, a coffin of lead, and one of wood. Forbidden for to open.

He went on, picking his words slowly, painfully, clearly.

So we opened it 'ere, in the cellar. One of our doctors was 'ere, for the autopsy. The young man 'e 'ad submitted the torture. They – (he gestured) – I cannot say it before a woman. And 'e 'ad not spoken, for others should have died. 'e was the son of old friends. I cannot 'elp your friend, mon caporal. *Je ne peux rien faire pour toi, ma pauvre fille.*

Belle pressed her hand tightly to her mouth – no gleaming orbs raised to heaven, but red eyelids and a snotty nose. Saul stood up suddenly and stood behind her, hands resting on her shoulders. The priest-soldier stood up too, and they faced each other over Belle's bowed head. The Frenchman still had that shy, almost apologetic look; Saul's heavy jaw was clamped tight with anger, against himself and his inarticulateness, against all the clever educated people who could talk and argue.

Look, Sir, he said slowly, I'm not clever and I can't beg. I'm sorry about your friend's boy. I don't think she had much choice really. I'm not asking she be let off, only for her to be kept safe till she can be tried properly, according to law.

She 'as been tried, said the priest. The judgement is passed.

You're a priest, said Saul, don't you believe in God's mercy?

I do not speak as a priest, I speak as a soldier. I 'ave orders.

You'll carry the guilt of this all your life, Sir.

You, Monsieur le Caporal, have you not killed?

I have, Sir, but that was fair fighting, against men.

'Ave you not killed young men, boys perhaps, with the gun, with the knife? (He glanced down at the broad knife at Saul's belt. There was a little silence.) You see, to be a soldier, it is to 'ave guilt, to carry guilt for others, all our lives. The guilt is necessary.

He went slowly and turned around to face them in the doorway.

Tu veux faire la confesse, ma pauvre enfant? he asked her.

She glanced up at Saul as if in explanation and shook her head. The doorway was empty and they could hear the officer's sharp footsteps retreating along the cloister.

Come on, girl, said Saul, let's get out. We're wasting our time here.

She got up quietly and obediently – no need to grasp her arm now. The old man came hobbling up and escorted them out; the gate clanged shut with finality behind them. The cloud was broken now with patches of blue, the hedgerows smelt of damp earth and the birds were singing. A flight of Spitfires roared in low and tailed off in the direction of the front.

Belle walked beside him in sullen silence.

Cheer up, girl, he said, I said I'd take care of you, and I will. You shan't be hurt, I promise.

The Church cannot save me, she said, do you think you can?

Yes, he said. It was so absurdly confident that she laughed bitterly, but it changed things, and the warm dank earth smelt of life after the bleak austerities of the abbey. He took her arm comfortably.

As I try to visualize the scene in the bleak visitors' room, to follow it back, track it through his eyes, decode it from his laconic speech, I am baffled. I can still hear the phrases he used – She was very quiet-like, you could see she didn't like it – This priest, I didn't take to him, he looked crafty, sort of. I can reconstruct the surface reality which they represent in a cryptic and oblique way. For example, when he called the soldier-priest 'crafty' he was translating the Frenchman's pain and embarrassment, for which he had no name, into a childhood Protestant stereotype.

I can see the pictures, and up to a point I can perhaps understand what they mean, the woman first sulking, then afraid, humiliated, angry, the priest's horror and revulsion. But both are also baffling – in spite of all, the woman's lack of shame, the priest's lack of compassion.

As I write this, it is just after eleven o'clock at night, and the transistor on my desk is carrying the BBC news for Monday 19 February 1973. The body of Marshal Pétain has been stolen from his felon's grave on the Ile d'Yeu by political resurrection-men, either to be tossed into the sea or to be reburied at Douaumont, in the haunted wasteland of Verdun. Either way it is sinister and strange, conjuring old ghosts, recalling old stories (as in Hans Chlumberg's play, *Miracle at Verdun*) of the war-dead rising in their thousands and marching back with rolling drums to accuse the living. Either way there will be no rest for the old hero, old traitor, though (my God) the Occupation of France is thirty years gone. (The Irish have remembered for three hundred years, the Jews for three thousand.) Some bitternesses never die. As she tried to tell him: You do not know, you should be glad you do not know.

As for Saul Scourby himself, perhaps he simply assumed that, since the woman and the priest were foreigners and Papists, their minds would be unintelligible to him, like their language. He waited patiently, as if in a solitary ambush, for something to move his way.

When they got back to the cottage, Charlie had cleaned up and brightened the fire in the stove, where the blackened kettle was starting to boil. As they entered the door, he had thrown open the grate and was blowing gently on the fire, so that the red-gold light of it lit up his thin pale face and faded blue eyes with a rich glow.

Wotcher, Charlie boy, said Saul.

Hullo, Corp, he said. Hullo, miss. I won't be long, the kettle's singing and I see you got some dry bread in the bin there so I'll make a nice bit of toast.

And he stabbed a slice on to a long kitchen-fork and held it steadily to the flames. Belle sat down slowly at the table and pulled off her head-scarf, letting her thick red hair fall loose around her shoulders. Saul unclipped the magazine from the sten, checked it over and quietly set it down by the dresser. He looked at the woman, who sat silent and still, watching Charlie at his domestic work. The first slice of toast was turned and finished and set down golden-brown on a plate. The kettle boiled and tea was made in the enamel coffee-pot. A second slice began to toast and the kitchen filled with the good dry smell.

Will you be mother, Corp? said Charlie. Sorry we ain't got no fresh milk. 'ave to use powdered. Don't taste the same without fresh milk. S'pose all the cows must've died round 'ere.

You wouldn't chuckle, said Saul, the fields are full of 'em, legs stuck up in the air. You mightn't believe it, but Charlie here is an expert on milk.

As he handed her the tea and toast, Belle broke off her introspective stare at the firelight and asked, Are you a farmer, Charlie?

Charlie laughed, a shy wheezy chuckle, at this small familiar joke.

No, miss, I'm a milkman. Or used to be, in civvy street, like. Back in 'ighgate, that's in London.

Did you have to get up early, she asked, and bring milk for the small breakfast? Such a hard life.

Oh, it's not bad, not bad at all. 'cept in winter perhaps. Dark they are, those winter mornings. More toast now – 'ere we are. Mind you, it used to be 'arder. When I was a nipper, I used to go round with my old man, 'e was a milkman too, on the old 'orsedrawn float. Going up the Archway Road in a winter fog, and the trams with their big 'eadlamps coming through the fog. Ladling out the milk from the big churns with the brass fittings. They stopped all that, said it was un-'ygeenic. It's all bottle stuff now.

His pinched pale face became animated as he talked, but suddenly he stopped as if embarrassed and busied himself with the fire and the toast, holding and turning it so that it was an exact golden-brown before slipping it steaming on to Belle's plate, to be eaten with margarine and plum jam from the ration-pack. As he crouched by the fire he glanced across shyly at Belle, at her long delicate fingers busy with knife and cup, at the rich red hair shaken out over her shoulders and catching highlights from the glow of the fire.

Watching them both, Saul realized with amusement that the little man was innocently and worshipfully in love with her. The tea and toast was a simple man's offering. He watched her all the time as they had their tea and chatted on about life as they had known it during the last years. British meeting French had this great curiosity for all the missing details, for knitting up the wholeness of ordinary life again. At last, he stood up and said, Well, time to be off, I s'pose. Oh, 'ere, I thought you might like these, I got plenty.

He took out three packets of Gold Flake and a bar of Cadbury's milk chocolate and laid them carefully on the scrubbed table in front of her. She smiled up at him with real enjoyment.

Thank you, Charlie – *vous êtes bien gentil* – you are very kind.

You're very welcome, I'm sure, he said, with a duck of the head, and bustled out of the door.

Saul walked with him up the path to the gate.

See you tomorrow, Corp, he said.

That's right, Charlie boy. And ta very much for everything.

Saul watched him as he trudged briskly up the hill, waving cheerfully as he passed the Brat, who was on watch under the big beech tree.

Some time must have passed then. I can guess at some of the many things he didn't tell me, but not all of them. He had a curious trick of saying things like: She often talked about her aunts in the country – or: There was this German airman, another one, who was after her to marry him, but she'd never tell me much about him – or: She used to sing to herself in a little voice, but tuneful, when she thought I wasn't listening – or: Sometimes we'd have terrible arguments over nothing much, like whether we wanted tea or coffee.

Sometimes it seemed as if he was talking about a woman he'd lived with for much longer than a weekend. There were those things he didn't elaborate, almost as if they were familiar daily details, accumulated over a long time. And when did she give him the twelve-franc copy of Baudelaire?

As she cleaned up, he went across the garden to the latrine. He carried his sten well in sight, and left the door of the little outhouse open. There were fighters about somewhere, and a slow-moving spotter-plane coming and going from a neighbouring field, and a bass engine-sound that sounded more like tanks on the move than trucks. As he walked back up the path quiet-footed, alert to all the sounds around him, perhaps he could hear her singing to herself in the kitchen, in that small voice:

> *Il me dit des mots d'amour*
> *Des mots de tous les jours*
> *Et ça m'fait quelque chose.*

But she stopped when she heard the click and tap of his boots on the path.

That's a nice orchard you got out there, he said. Normandy's famous for apples, isn't it?

Yes, she said, still at the sink, but they are not yet ripe. The harvest will be good at the end of the summer.

Then she stopped, and they both were thinking that there would be time for many things before the apples were heavy on the trees – love, death, even the end of a war.

Come outside for a while, he said.

She turned and looked at him, wary, puzzled.

Come on, he said, the rain's over. Come out and get some air. Nothing's going to hurt you.

She went over to the kitchen dresser and began to tie back her heavy bronze hair with a piece of blue ribbon, watching her reflection in a small mirror propped up on the shelf among the cups. The movement of her raised arms lifted her big breasts under the thin blouse and this excited him. He stepped up quietly behind her and slid his hands up her sides and across her chest, holding her firmly while he pressed his face against her neck. Her hair fell loose again as she lowered her arms, pulled back against him to ease his grip, and twisted around in his arms. She faced him, flushed, flattered, a little angry. He promptly kissed her, close and open-mouthed. She responded to him warmly, but twisted her mouth free.

No, she said sulkily.

Why not? he said. You could fancy it, couldn't you?

No, she said. Not like this. I like to be asked.

D'you mean the Jerries asked for it, all polite-like?

Most, she said, they were *comme il faut*, nice. Not all, but most. Those I liked.

So you don't like me?

Let me choose, Saul, I could like you. Let us walk in the orchard.

She finished tying up her hair. They walked out of

the front door; the sky was full of broken cloud, and the light brightened and faded. Up the hill a broad shaft of sunlight spotlit the beech tree and the solitary figure beneath it like a stage set.

See, she said as they stood in the orchard, it will be a good summer for the apples.

The boughs were thick with the small hard green lumps which had once been blossom. After the rain it was dank under the trees, in the long grass, with a smell of green rawness and rankness. He listened, half expecting a sound of bees; but there was only the small heavy drone of a bumble-bee, drowned in the sound of a convoy of trucks changing gear and grinding up the hill.

Then something happened quite suddenly and unexpectedly, at least by that time in Normandy, when the daytime skies were the unchallenged beat of the Hurricane and the Spitfire. A roar of aircraft suddenly surged up out of the fields and along the line of the road. Saul jerked his head up at the shadowy shapes that flashed by above the orchard trees. At the same time gunfire chattered in the air and scattered, surprised shots answered from the ground.

Saul's reactions were delayed for a few seconds by surprise, before he caught Belle round the waist and flung her to the ground, with his body shielding her. The raiders circled tightly and roared in again, with more gunfire. Splinters buzzed and clipped and whickered through the trees. Then it was all gone.

She was lying close against him, her face pressed

against his shoulder. As the noise died away, she raised her head slowly, looking at him and not smiling. He kept holding her close and began to kiss her, she trying to push him away, gently at first. Nothing was said. He shifted himself, holding her down with his heavy body across hers. His hand moved down and lifted her skirt. Silently she fought him, as if they must both make no sound in case they were overheard by some prowling enemy. Silently he pinioned her arms back in a ruthless grip and tugged at her clothing and his own, until he could roll over on top of her. She hissed with rage as he took her quickly, sorrowfully. To dominate her had become the only thing that mattered, and he had little pleasure of it.

When he pulled back from her he was slow and wary, as if expecting her to attack him with fists or nails. Instead, she lay back in the trampled grass, pulling down her rumpled skirt which had twisted up around her waist and staring up at him in shame and rage. But when she spoke her voice was flat and expressionless.

You dirty English pig, she said, no Boche did that to me.

I bet, he said.

Not like that, she said. That is the first time I have been raped.

I bet, he said.

Yes, you bet, she said with sudden passion. I have been bad, yes, I have been a *putain*, but I make good love and I give pleasure. I can be good to a man. But not to you. You want to do it all for yourself. The woman to you is for nothing.

She scrambled to her feet, still fumbling to put her clothes to rights and with her copper hair hanging loose about her face. He lay sprawled on the grass and squinted up at her with a shaft of sunlight behind her.

You are just the bull who wants the cow.

She thrust out her clenched right fist and chopped her left hand across her right forearm in a universal and explicit gesture which startled him, for he had the old-fashioned working-class puritanism about how a woman should speak and behave, regardless of what else had just happened.

He propped his back against one of the apple trees, smoking and staring out at the shifting sunlight. I knew it wasn't right, he said to me afterwards in his flat understated way, I shouldn't of done it like that, without kindness. But I think it was more than that: in the post-coital sadness he judged himself coldly and saw himself as a fool who had thrown away a chance of true joy. Yet he knew it wasn't intended: sudden closeness had undone him, the desire to protect had turned into the need to possess.

He was feeling sullen and ashamed, unwilling to meet her, and thinking that she would be in the kitchen or the bedroom, he walked slowly to the other entrance at the back of the house, and pushed open the top half of the Dutch door.

What he saw there was surprising and, in a way,

beautiful. The back door opened into the scullery and wash-house, floored with flagstones. At one side was a copper, set in a brick frame and chimney. On the other was a wooden washtub on three legs and a barrel which was kept filled with water brought in, bucket by bucket, from the pump in the garden. Water could be dippered from the barrel for the copper or the wooden washtub, and spillage ran out through a drain-hole set in the flagstones.

Belle was standing naked in the middle of the wash-house. She must have pulled off her blue-and-white dress and her underwear and flung it in a heap in the corner. She had soaped herself at the tub, scrubbing fiercely at her body which shone pink and as if varnished with soapsuds. Now she stood there with her back to him and with her arms stretched straight up, holding one of the heavy buckets filled with water above her head. She seemed to be full of fury and sudden strength, so that the smooth womanly muscles of her arms and shoulders, back and buttocks, thighs and calves were braced tightly as she balanced the bucket and tipped it. The water, cold from the barrel on the flagstones, cascaded down over her head and body, and poured out down the drain-hole. She cried out, a small gasping scream, at the shock, and the emptied bucket crashed to the flagstones.

In the following silence the door creaked and she looked back over her shoulder and saw him standing there. With a startled movement she grabbed for the crumpled dress and held it up to cover herself.

Go away, she said, do not watch me.

Sorry, he muttered, embarrassed and a little re-pelled, I didn't mean – Then, taking in the bareness of the room, he said, Where's your towel?

It does not matter, she said crossly.

Wait, he said, and went quickly round the side of the cottage to the front garden. He'd had a good new towel in his pack and had put it out to dry on the hedge, catching the afternoon sunlight. This he brought back for her. She was still standing there half covered with her crumpled dress, so he hung the towel over the half-door.

There you are, he said, you'll need that.

And she thanked him, watching him with an embarrassed smile at the absurdity of it.

He went back again round the outside of the house towards the front door. The rain had blown over, leaving the low sun warm in a clear late-afternoon sky, where a flight of Spitfires was making regular sweeps towards the German lines.

He switched on the radio and went back to sit in the open doorway and smoke. There was a Forces Requests programme on; he found it dull and paid little atten-tion, sitting there brooding and staring out at the landscape. Trees and hedges and low hills were be-ginning to take on a shadowy impenetrable look against the brightening western sky. He could not quite make out the figure of the watcher under the beech tree until the small flash of sunlight reflected on spectacles showed that it was the old man. He finished his cigarette, flipped the butt into the garden and began to dismantle his sten gun and clean its worn immaculate metalwork with an oily rag. He liked to have his gear in perfect working order, and besides, it might help to impress anyone who happened to be watching.

(Of such small actions is war made. And this is the part that most war books get wrong. Trying hard to impress, they multiply the horror and glory, brutality and heroism, boredom and humour of war at the expense of its ordinariness. Most wars are just ordinary. Everyone, even in the worst of wars, must sleep about a third of each day, and eat two or three meals, and crap even if it's only in a hole in the ground. Soldiers, like anyone else, catch colds and read the *Daily Mirror* and fall in love and trim their nails and play pontoon and listen to Frank Sinatra and change their socks. The sadness of wartime death and suffering is that they are embedded in these familiar things.)

Presently she came in from the back of the house and began to move about in the kitchen. There was a scrape and rattle at the stove as she opened the grate and stirred the fire. He said nothing, but his hands were busily cleaning and refilling the spare magazines. When he had finished he put the magazines, with the cleaning gear, back in the pouch on his webbing belt and stood up, slinging it loose over his shoulder.

He walked over softly and stopped behind her where

she stood at the stove, stooping a little, stirring something in the enamel pot which began to have a savoury meaty smell.

I'm sorry, Belle, he said. Truly, love. You were so close to me, I couldn't stop. I didn't mean to harm you.

She remained with her back to him, stirring angrily at the black pot, saying nothing.

I said I'm sorry, he said, like I told you, I don't take a girl if she don't want it.

How can I choose? she said. Do not worry. I am disposable as you wish. And I will cook your supper.

Be a good girl, he said patting her bottom under the thin green dress.

She wriggled away from him, still angry but willing to be pleased.

He went through the little passage into the bedroom, leaving both doors open. His pack stood neat and square against the wall, and he unbuckled it and took out the bottle of Calvados. He shook it and held it up to the light; still half full.

Glancing down, he took in her dressing-table set in front of the window, with its litter of woman's gear – pots and tubes and bottles, dabs of cotton wool, some stained with rouge or mascara, a good pair of silver-backed brushes – he knew the quality – with strands of long red-gold hair caught among the bristles. There was a small stand-mirror and, caught in the frame, a photograph.

He slipped it out and looked at it. It was just a snapshot, but taken with some skill, and it showed the head and shoulders of a middle-aged man. The setting seemed to be a garden – at least, there was a blurred shape of trees in the background. He thought that the man must be quite old because there was grey in the hair and in the thick drooping moustache, but even more because of the suggestion of heaviness in the jowls and in what could be seen of the body. There was character in it, arrogance in the tilt of the thrown-back head and the folded droop of the eyelids – or was it just the glare of the afternoon sun?

Back in the kitchen, he found her sitting at the table, arms folded under her breasts, staring down listlessly at nothing. From the sideboard he took two large wine glasses and poured a generous tot of Calvados into each one.

Here, he said, try this.

To his astonishment, she took the glass and immediately raised it to her mouth and knocked the drink straight back in a curiously man-like gesture. She didn't even cough, and went back to staring at the table.

Here, he said, you'll do yourself an injury that way, my girl.

He sat down beside her at the table. Reaching out his right hand he gently touched her under the chin and forced her to look up. Her clear eyes were reddened and watery, and he grinned at her.

Don't you do that too often, he said, or those beautiful eyes of yours will stay permanently bloodshot. Look at you, you're a mess.

Pouring her a much smaller drink, he pushed it across and lit a cigarette for her.

Now drink that slow, he said, and I'll join you.

He sipped the dark golden liquid, feeling the fire of it travel down his throat.

Otherwise, he went on, you might wind up like an old bloke my grandad told me about, what lived on smuggled brandy – that was far back in the days of smuggling from France – from here. Regular pickled in it, he was. Well, one night he went to blow out the candle as he was off to bed, and true as I'm here, he caught fire and blew up. Straight, he wrecked a whole row of cottages. Local people talk about it to this day.

She gave a sniff of unwilling laughter, sipped her drink, drew on her cigarette and stared again at the table. He slid the snapshot across to her.

Who's this? he said.

My father.

I thought so. Got your nose. Dead?

Yes.

Germans?

No, she said, but after a long hesitation, as if she wasn't sure.

What's his name?

Alcibiade.

What?

Alcibiade. She anglicized it for him, Alcibiades.

Odd name, sounds Greek.

He was a Greek and a sort of hero. My father used to

tell me about him, he was proud of the name, my father. Alcibiade lived in Athens, and he was very rich and a crook and when he was young he was – you say, 'queer'? – and had many lovers.

She drained her glass with a little animated gesture. He silently poured her another and passed her another cigarette.

Well, you know, Athens and Sparta had a big war, like France and Germany, and there was the King of Persia too, waiting, like Stalin. Alcibiade was good at war, so when the Spartans tried to make a peace he sabotaged it and went on fighting them. But presently he got into much trouble for some kind of sacrilege at Athens, and the priests cursed him, so he ran away and fought for the Spartans. He was a collaborator, you see. But he really had fear of no one. He slept with the Spartan king's wife, and this made the king very angry. So he went back to Athens and won more battles for them. But in the end they lost, and the Spartans were the winners, like the Boches with us. So Alcibiade ran away to Persia. No one wanted him now. So one night the Persian king sent soldiers to surround the house where he lived. He was living with a whore, a woman who had been taken a slave in one of the wars. So there he was in bed with her, and the soldiers came and set fire to the house. But he was still a brave man. He wrapped a cloak around one arm and took his sword and he was all naked and he jumped through the fire. The soldiers were still afraid of him – imagine, one naked man – then they shot into him with arrows and spears till he died. Then his woman sold her jewels and her good dress – you know, every whore has one good dress – and she paid for his funeral.

Who paid for hers? he said.

She shrugged and stared down at the table and her empty glass. He refilled it and said: That was a good story.

It means that all wars are the same, she said.

The long sunlight was beginning to slide in underneath the clouds. He rose to his feet.

I'll just take a turn outside, he said. That smells good, he added, nodding at the stove.

The pots on the stove heaved and hissed. She jumped up and ran over to them and began to lift lids and peer inside and test something with a spoon and take everything off the heat because it was cooking too fast. The sad sulky woman turned into a busy housewife.

Do not be too long, she said, soon the dinner will be cooked.

At intervals, while writing Saul Scourby's story, I have been re-reading Alfred de Vigny's *Servitude et Grandeur Militaires* and thinking about it. He was too young to serve in Napoleon's armies and in any case he was a Royalist – he did his service in the post-war army sworn loyal to the Bourbons. But he had an extraordinary sympathy and understanding for those men who had grown old in Napoleon's endless wars, and for what he called their 'abnegation' – their selfless lives of duty and poverty, like some fighting monastic order. Listen:

Well, during the fourteen years I spent in the army it was there only, and above all in the poor despised ranks of the infantry, that I found men of this classic stamp, men who carry the sentiment of duty to its ultimate consequences, feeling neither remorse for their obedience nor shame for their poverty, simple in manner and speech, proud of the fame of their country, while careless of their own, happy in their obscurity, and in sharing with the unfortunate the black bread they purchase with their blood.

I've known men like that, especially among regular army NCOs. Saul was not the same. His patriotism was a tribal attachment to his own place; he was poor because he needed little beyond the satisfaction of his immediate needs; and his love of obscurity was the hunting animal's instinctive preference for shadow and silence. But he knew how to share the black bread of bitterness in his own way, as you'll see later.

When he came back to the kitchen, the dinner was ready. She had taken tinned potatoes, sliced them and poached them in reconstituted milk with shredded cheese to make a sort of *gratin dauphinois*. The tinned steak-and-kidney pudding had been taken apart and remade into a delicious stew with dumplings. There was still some cheese left over to go with biscuits and the usual ersatz coffee.

He praised her cooking and lapsed into what was, for him, an unusual silence. The woman's contempt for him after the scene in the orchard, her measuring him up against her other lovers (no Boche did that to me), made him still angry and (rare thing) unsure of how to go on. He could have slung his kit and moved off, but after all he'd promised to take care of her till Monday morning, and she was entitled to count on that. His word was passed on it and besides, another day was another world, full of its own possibilities.

Looking up he saw that she had propped her father's photograph on the sideboard – even at the distance, he could see the family resemblance in that arrogant set of the head. Her eyes followed his, and she said: Do you want to know about him?

If you like, he said, if you – that is, he's dead, isn't he? Like you told me. You don't have to say any more, you know.

I wish you to understand, she said patiently, about the Germans. That is what killed him, at last.

While she talked she went on doing her chores, clearing the table and setting out the blue cups and making another pot of the bad ersatz coffee, her capable hands working away as it were on their own, quite separate from her sad brooding mind.

Once things had settled down with the Germans – this was where it all started, back in the summer of nineteen-forty – the old people were resigned but young people like the ones she knew were pleasantly excited by all these Germans, young, vigorous, free-spending, above all victorious. For her father things had been hard at first, because the firm for which he travelled had been taken over for war-production. But then there was a shortage of young men about, so many rounded up or missing after the débâcle of June, and soon her father was able to take quite a good post in the syndicate of municipal transport. She was working too, as *vendeuse* in the big store, Au Printemps.

At first the young German soldiers and the young French girls went by, eyeing one another and smiling at one another in the streets and squares. All the good, well-brought-up young girls, that is. There were the other kind, of course, the girls down round the docks; the conquerors found ready welcome there.

It was in July, as the long evenings began to shorten a little, that she was out walking with two friends near the little park some way from her home. The three of them often went out together because they complemented one another and, as women know, that is very flattering – one, Marie, a pale blonde, one, Yvonne, very dark, herself, Belle, a lustrous copper-head. Young German soldiers often looked at them appreciatively and longingly as they swung in step along the boulevards, watchful, provocative, caring for no man. The soldiers would hail them in broken French: *Bonsoir mamzelle, vous promenade mit mir?*

This time it was different. A very beautiful Mercedes purred up alongside and kept pace with them, and a voice asked in good French whether the gracious ladies would be kind to three lonely pilots. Everything would be quite as it should be, just to drive into the country, to an inn near the river, to take a glass of wine and then return just as they wished.

She turned to the agreeable voice and found herself looking straight at the driver of the car, this young fair-haired airman with eyes as blue as flax-flowers. With him, one beside him and the other in the back of the open car, were his two friends, both handsome, both dark (they were playing the same trick, but he was the one who showed to advantage by it), all in the smart blue-grey uniform of the Luftwaffe, with smiles like a private uniform too.

Marie and Yvonne held back, but she, always the bold one, stepped forward and smiled at the fair-haired airman. No, they were very kind but, it was late, people might talk –

But what harm – ? no one need recognize them, soon it would be dark, the inn was very tranquil.

Still she hesitated, turned back, argued with her friends in broken sentences and shrugs and giggles. Still Marie and Yvonne held back and the young Germans waited, smiling, putting in encouraging words.

Then she, Belle, suddenly stepped up to the car, and the dark young man on the inside front jumped out and helped her in, sitting between the two of them in front, while her friends took their places on each side of the third young man in the back. There was much blushing and giggling. Then the blond driver put his foot down and the beautiful car roared off up the boulevard and presently the streets fell behind and the country breeze tossed their hair, copper, pale and black.

The driver's name was Gustav Schellenberg; the other beside her was Karl Altmann, and the quiet one in the back was Rudi something. So they drove out into the country and drank champagne at an inn by the river. Rudi played the piano and the young men sang together in clear loud German voices, while the locals kept away from them and stared and muttered. When they drove back the harvest moon was out, Belle found herself alone in the front seat with Gustav, while the other four squeezed in the back, all very friendly.

After that they went on meeting, three and three, near the little park, when they could, not every day, for the young pilots were stationed somewhere near Rennes, and sometimes when they were on duty they came in too late to get away for the evening.

The days shortened; the summer glory faded; the young faces, looked at by loving eyes, began to show tired lines; the radios playing '*Wir Fahren Gegen England*' began to have a jaunty and slightly desperate sound. One evening in September, as the nights began to chill, they saw only two heads in the approaching car, and Rudi something wasn't there. After that dark

Yvonne didn't come out with them any more; they met two and two.

There was a small, quiet hotel overlooking the river at Vernon, where they went regularly. The patron and his wife were servile, obsequious, well paid. They went there at first to drink and talk as before, then, naturally enough, to keep a couple of rooms, and spend long afternoons together when they could.

One afternoon, as they drove up to the hotel, she noticed a man staring at them from the little terrace of the hotel. He had a square red face and grey hair *en brosse* and gold-rimmed glasses, and with him was an ugly woman, no doubt his wife. Only (by an odd flash of memory) as Gustav took her in the bed did she remember the red face and the glasses as Monsieur Beauvoisin, her father's boss. Hours later, when they came out, of course the ugly couple were gone.

At the end of the week her father came home early, looking old and very grey. He had been curtly dismissed by Monsieur Beauvoisin, whose son had lost an arm at Calais, and who thus had a better claim on the job – he was, after all, a *grand mutilé de guerre*, while Belle's father was a mere *ancien combattant*.

But another job was available, behind the counter in a post office, smaller, poorer, but enough for him to hold his head up and, as winter drew in, to go down in his shabby overcoat to the café on the square, to meet old friends and spin out frugal cups of coffee and play dominoes and checkers with other *anciens combattants*, for a time. Then Monsieur Beauvoisin must have talked to someone who talked to someone.

One night – it was early in the New Year, of nineteen-forty-one, that is – he went to the café as usual. And then, as he walked in and the door swung to behind him, into the room full of yellow light and steam and the smell of Gauloises, the talk stopped. People, his friends, looked at him strangely, sideways He sat down at one of the marble-topped tables. Guyot was sitting there, whom he had known since the lycée, with the checkers set out before him, the white pieces politely turned towards the chair opposite, waiting for a game. Papa hung up the shabby overcoat and sat down thankfully in the empty wooden chair, easing off the old galoshes which hurt his feet (there was slush on the pavements outside). With a familiar gesture he reached out and made the first move, looking down at the board. A chair ground on the tiles. Without a word, Guyot stood up and walked away to another table.

He had to call the boy, who came reluctantly and brought his coffee, and stood near him, obviously eager to take the cup as soon as it seemed to be empty. No one spoke, dominoes clicked on the marble; the urns hissed. The patron watched him silently over the counter, slowly polishing the zinc top.

He put on the old coat and galoshes and went home. When he tried to tell Belle about it – it happened to be a night when she was at home – he was neither hurt nor angry, only immensely astonished and shivering with cold. She left him sitting by the small gas-heater while she went into the kitchen to make him a good *tisane* of herbs. There was a sound like a dry cough and something fell. Hurrying back to the sitting-room she found him huddled against the side of his tall chair, the arrogant head sunk, the face drawn down at one side in a fixed, mechanical sneer.

Luckily the stroke was a light one; the job went, of course, but soon he could limp around the apartment with a stick. Belle could still get out; she was good at her job and she could claim (sometimes with truth) that she was working overtime. A near neighbour, a widow who had liked her father, could come in and sit with him – Belle thought that perhaps she knew what had happened at the café, but she came all the same. Belle herself began to get some odd looks around the *quartier*, in the shops, at the market. But the women were more cautious than the men; after all, some of them had daughters too, and in any case who would want to offend someone with a powerful German friend? Papa's income was missed, but Gustav was kind and generous, and gave her thoughtful presents – delicacies, good winter clothing, some discreet jewellery.

He had always been very considerate, dropping the girls off far enough from their homes, but in time to catch one of the late trams. Late snow came, and moonlight. One afternoon she met Gustav alone; Karl was on duty, so Marie had stayed sulkily at home.

Because they were alone they were especially loving to each other. Afternoon merged with early winter dusk, and later, when she awoke from a light sleep beside him, it was nearly nine. They dressed and hurried out to the car and she settled down beside him, relaxed but a little breathless, as the car streamed through the night back to the city in the bright moonlight, with a powdering of snow on the bare fields, while below the horizon the searchlights danced over England.

Because it was so late, because with the moonlight, the cold, the wine and the love they were very lightly and ethereally drunk, they forgot the usual discretion and stopped right by the entrance that led into the courtyard of Belle's apartment house. She kissed him standing there in the bright moonlight, and waved after him as the Mercedes roared away.

Inside the house it was all dark. Letting herself in with her key, she tapped on her father's bedroom door and called quietly to him in case he was still awake, but there was no answer, so she went to bed and dreamed that she was having tea with her father in the teashop in the Rue de l'Horloge.

Next morning, huddled in her dressing-gown, she got up to make the coffee. The way to the kitchenette lay through the little salon, and when she opened the door she saw at once the crumpled figure lying on the floor by the window. The curtains were parted, and a long narrow streak of pale snow-reflected light lay across the room and the fallen body like a ruler. He must have put out the light and opened the curtains when he heard the Mercedes draw up outside, and everything must have been very bright and sharp in the moonlight, framed in the entrance to the court-yard.

It was also the last time she saw Gustav. Marie heard from Karl that he was missing over England, then reported wounded, a prisoner. After a while she went back to work, but didn't go out much for months. She lost touch with Marie and Karl, but she thought that they had been going together until Karl was sent east for Operation Barbarossa in the summer of 'forty-one

Now again I've been recreating what Saul understood of what she'd remembered and told him, refining and reinforcing and enhancing those fogged photographs from the past. And all the time the room darkened around them in the summer twilight and she made more coffee and outside the German bombers swept in over the distant bay and the slow silent streams of incandescent tracer seemed to float up into the dark sky.

When she finished they tried the electricity but as usual it was off, so she drew the curtains and lit a candle. They opened the grate of the stove and they sat staring into the dying red glow, smoking and saying little. He watched her unmoving profile. In the oblique light from the fire the early hidden signs of age developed like a photographic plate – the wrinkles moulded around the eyes, the set lines of the upper lip, the beginnings of heaviness under the chin. Presently she yawned and went off to the bedroom, taking the candle; he finished his cigarette and followed her.

After what had passed between them in the orchard that afternoon it might seem she would be cold to him, even not want him at all. But he could be a patient and wise listener when he wished to be, and he had listened to her story with only the kind of interruptions that showed interest and concern. Talking of her first German lover had eased her, and she was responsive enough to rouse him at once when he blew out the candle and stripped and lay down beside her in the big bed in the dark.

Why do you put out the light? she said. Am I ugly? Do you not wish to see me?

You're all right, he said, I mean really all right. I like to see you in the daylight.

My face, my hands. Not my body. Is my body ugly?

She was teasing him, but it struck on an obscure nerve, and he began to lose his potency.

It's not you, he said awkwardly, it's something else. It just doesn't seem right, to look on a woman's nakedness, to uncover a man's parts. It's not right, that's all.

Uh, you English are hypocrites, Puritans.

What about you French?

The same. I know.

What about the Germans?

She turned sharply away from him and he heard her breath catch.

Gustav loved to look at me, she said, in the bedroom at the inn. The light came in from the garden. The leaves made shadows on the bed. He said that love should be made out of doors – in nature. By the light of the sun, he said, the eye of Apollo, or the light of the full moon, the eye of Diana.

And did you?

How could we, with all those spying people? But he was so beautiful, Apollo's son. He too fell out of the sky, you know.

The classical talk bored and puzzled him, and he lay on his back staring at the darkness. She turned back to him with one of her sudden changes of mood.

Not like you, she said. You are dark and cruel, you belong to the darkness.

She beat her fist gently against the flat hard muscles of his chest.

You go in the dark, she said, to kill, to steal, to make love.

That's right, he said in surprise. I've always liked night-time. I grew up in the country, without street-lamps. I like to hide and watch. That's why I was a good hunter.

Then things began to go right again, as he turned towards her and drew her close. When he readied himself and went into her it was (in his own words) like a torchlight procession with brass bands. As they separated again, getting their breath, there was a sudden flurry of gunfire not far away, answered by a distant one from the Germans and followed by the muffled noise of incoming shells. It went on for some time, perhaps a counter-battery exercise, perhaps a luckless patrol caught in the open between the lines and hammered.

He slept deeply and struggled up out of a confused dream in which his granny was showing him the big *Pilgrim's Progress* book with the pictures. They came to the one she always passed over quickly, but this time he held her hand and made her stay. It was the page where Christian was shown in the Valley of the Shadow, twined in struggle with Apollyon – Christian in his armour, scaly Apollyon bat-winged and fiery-eyed. The picture filled him with an old fear and he struggled with it formlessly and awoke to find that it was Belle who was groaning and throwing herself about like a sick animal in its throes. He pulled her against him and held her close. It was some time before she knew where she was, coming out of a kind of delirium into the warmth of the bed, and still panting, with sweat on her body, as if she had been running desperately away from some terror.

He talked to her all the while as he might to a frightened horse or dog.

There now, girl, there's a good girl now, there's nothing to fear, I've got you, old Saul's got you, ah there's a sorry girl to cry out so, don't cry now, Saul's got you, you'll come to no harm, that's a pretty girl, be quiet now, don't carry on so, there's nothing to fear.

On and on, while she sweated and trembled against him and her breathing grew calmer until she heaved a deep sigh and was quiet.

That was a bad one, wasn't it? he said, and she nodded her head in the dark.

Yes, she said, oh yes.

What were you dreaming of, girl? Tell me now and get rid of it. Then you'll sleep.

I dreamed, she said, about the prison in Rouen where they put Jeanne D'Arc. It is like a prison cell, but open all round. There were soldiers there all the time, she was never to herself, imagine, she could not even cover herself to go to the *pissoire*. Imagine that, like an animal. Then she was burned.

She stopped and he prompted her.

So you were Joan of Arc, in the dream? he said.

No, she hesitated, no, but like. I was in a cell but like a hospital room and with windows all round. Men watching me, Gestapo. And I was to be taken and burned. I thought how it would hurt me, and then I thought, it is like the dentist, a time shall be when it shall be finished, no more pain. If I could reach that time – but first there will be the pain of the fire.

She was silent again.

Go on, he said gently.

But that was the dream.

Oh sure, but that's not all, is it? Why do you dream about the Gestapo?

Everyone in France has dreamed about the Gestapo, from time to time.

Why you specially? What have they done to you, girl?

Nothing.

But they threatened you or something, didn't they? And it joins up with them blokes under the tree, don't it? Come on, tell me, girl. You'll feel better.

Saul's rough and ready psychoanalysis was genuine enough, and a man versed in country matters could know that the mind too has need of its purges. But he was also curious, in a detached way, and again he felt, despite himself, a sense of involvement and, uncomfortably, jealousy.

So she told him. After Gustav had gone and her father had died she had lived very much to herself for a while. A good-looking girl could always pick up another German soldier, but she had not wished to. Instead, she began going around with French youngsters of her own generation – some distant cousins, people she had known at school, friends of theirs. They hadn't known about her German lover, or had forgotten, or didn't care. One she came to know well – he had a beautiful name, 'Balthazar'. Soon they became lovers, and they would meet in a little hotel by the docks where sailors took their women, renting rooms by the hour. Balthazar seemed to be on good terms with the heavy dark woman who owned it – he called her 'tante', and she might have been his real aunt, for all Belle knew. They could always get a room there.

She liked it because it was full of dark corridors and strange smells of spices and toilets. Some of the foreign sailors smoked hashish, even in wartime – she tried it once and was sick. Dirty half-dressed girls stood in half-opened doorways, with glimpses of towsled heads behind them and tattooed men buckling on their trousers. There was always noise in the corridors – whispering, laughter, singing, sometimes cries and screams. A huge one-eyed old man with a terrible seamed face acted as bouncer and two small boys in dirty white coats scurried about the corridors on endless errands, bringing water and towels and cups of coffee, bottles of wine and crusty sandwiches from the bistro next door. It excited her because it was dark and strange and louche, and she liked Balthazar because he was at home there.

One spring evening when they met, he took her arm and steered her into the bistro instead of into the entrance to the hotel. They sat over their coffees in the little bar, silent and ill at ease.

There was something he must tell her, he did not wish it, please understand. He did not know – had she had German friends, a lover perhaps?

Yes, it is true, but why –

Then I must not – we must not meet again.

But why – it is all over now. He is a prisoner in England. Please –

No, do not think it is my feelings. I am not the jealous type, one should be above such things. (He was a boy who said things like that.) If it was up to me –

Why then – who told you? Who is making you?

Please, Belle, do not meet me again. Forget me, forget this place, everything. Believe me, it is really dangerous.

They went out into the chilly spring evening and he walked with her in silence to the tram. They parted with a coldly formal handshake.

Then she met this girl Thérèse who came in to share the apartment, and she had a lover in the SS and he had a friend, and that was how Belle met her SS lover who told her about the reprisals in Poland. By this time the Germans had invaded Russia. At first there had been the same excited feeling as in the previous summer. The SS, Hitler's supermen, were a very special breed, and being accepted as one of their women drafted her into a kind of club, where she shared in a small way the mystique, the confidence, the triumph.

Winter came. Nothing was actually said, but they knew something was wrong, because all the beautiful young Germans began to be posted away to the eastern front, and their places were taken by older and grimmer men. She became the mistress of a big grey powerful man, a colonel in some kind of staff job, not a field-officer. She feared him but felt safe with him, a secure immovable man who seemed to embody for her all the power of the Reich. His name was Emil Winterhalter but she referred to him always as Winterhalter. Yet he was kind to her, was proud of her beauty and bought her good clothes and enjoyed showing her off at parties.

One day in early spring, again, she had driven with him into the country. It was still very cold, and on the way back he told the driver to pull up at a café so that they could go in for a hot grog. As she sat down and loosened the tall fur collar of her winter coat – one of his presents – she looked up and found the waiter staring at her over Winterhalter's shoulder. For a moment she did not recognize him; it was Balthazar, looking gaunt and older. He put his fingers to his lips in a fumbling please-keep-silence gesture, which he covered by pretending to cough. He hurried away, and his place was taken by an older man who served their orders. Winterhalter seemed not to have noticed, but he watched her thoughtfully, almost tenderly, from his hooded grey eyes as she drank her grog. Before they left, he politely excused himself and made a phone call.

On their way back through the twilit streets, he said: I should like to stop here and introduce you to an old friend of mine. Do not worry, it will not take long.

They drew up by a house with a courtyard. If it had been full daylight she might have recognized it, for it was well known, but in near-darkness all she could think was that it reminded her of home, the apartment overlooking a cobbled yard and grey buildings. But here, instead of a *concierge* in black with a shawl, they were carefully covered with

Schmeissers and inspected before Colonel Winterhalter was recognized and saluted and the car passed through the gateway.

He guided her, not through the main door, but down stone steps and through a kitchen-basement entrance at the side of the yard. There was a long whitewashed corridor and two men lounging by a stove. They straightened up as Winterhalter came in and one of them spoke to him, pointing to a telephone.

Excuse me, my dear, he said, a small task I must attend to. Follow this man, he will take you to the reception-room.

And he nodded to one of them, a short thick man in a leather jacket, and with a broad face cratered with old acne scars. She followed him along the corridor and round a corner. He flung open a metal-sheathed door and she entered, expecting to find herself in a service-lift. Instead, she was standing at the entrance to a small windowless high-ceilinged room lit by an unshaded bulb. It was strangely decorated with what at first sight appeared to be a light buff wallpaper speckled all over in red-brown. In the middle of the opposite wall a rough outline of a human body with upstretched arms seemed to be silhouetted in buff with streaks of brown.

The man pushed her ungently in the back and she stumbled three steps into the room. The light swayed, and she saw the manacles hanging from ring-bolts high up on the wall, and all the whitewashed walls of the dirty room streaked and speckled with dried blood.

The light swung faster and faster, there was a roaring whisper in her ears and she felt the vomit rising in her throat. Before she could fall, Colonel Winterhalter was there, gently supporting her, leading her out of the dreadful little room, shouting something not very angry at the stocky man who slouched off grinning.

Forgive me, my dear, he said soothingly, a most terrible mistake. I reproach myself – the man is stupid and new here – I meant him to take you to my friend's reception-room upstairs.

And this time it was the service-lift, from which they stepped out again on to soft carpets and through a panelled door into a warm rich softly-lit room that smelled of woodfires and coffee and good cigars. The man who rose from the polished desk to greet them was tall and thin and old, dressed in soft grey tweeds. He spoke to them gently, like a nice old professor, as Colonel Winterhalter explained about the unpleasant mistake, and the old man offered her a glass of good brandy and settled her comfortably in a leather chair beside the desk.

Gently, diffidently, he pushed forward a photograph which lay in the circle of lamp-light on the desk. She stared at it stupidly. It was a snapshot taken somewhere on the boulevards and probably by a concealed camera. Against the blurred background, it showed quite clearly three young men walking along together.

One she did not know; one she vaguely remembered; the third was Balthazar.

We should like a little help from you, mamzelle, explained the older man in good French. This young man, you know him, I think? (He glanced at Winterhalter, who nodded, smiling.) Of course. Now he has been a little foolish. He has fallen into bad company. We should like to talk to him, to warn him. But (he chuckled kindly) we do not know where to find him. Young people are so restless, the *Wanderjahre*, we all know, don't we? So if you could just tell us where we could find him – an address, a favourite café, perhaps?

She emptied her brandy glass but it did not help. She went on staring at the photograph, her mind full of blank misery. Balthazar was saying something, something funny, the other two young faces were turned to him, smiling.

Be gentle, doctor, said the Colonel softly, our young friend has had a shock. She was shown – by mistake, of course – into the interrogation-room.

What a pity, said the older man, what a pity.

The Colonel laid his hands lightly on her shoulders and the touch shot like an electric shock through her body. She heard her voice come out dry and cracked like a prisoner under torture: I do not know – I know only one thing. A hotel where we – where he used to stay.

And then she told them the address.

The Colonel helped her to a big soft armchair over

in the dark corner of the room away from the lamp-light. Far away she could hear the older man speaking in rapid German on the telephone. The room grew very dim and she must have dozed.

When she woke up, the window curtains were open; Winterhalter and the Gestapo man were looking down into the courtyard outside. They talked in low voices; Winterhalter laughed. She caught the word 'Alésia'. She stood up uncertainly and came behind them, dazed and curious. Two army trucks were backed into the courtyard and there was a heavy guard. A spotlight was switched on. The backs of the trucks were thrown open; the prisoners inside were pushed out, sprawling on the cobbles, picked up, dragged inside. Some of them seemed to be unconscious. One of them was Balthazar; one was Wolf-face's godson; one was the Brat's cousin; one was the boy from the village.

Saul didn't necessarily believe all of this story – as he said later, he only had her word for it. That may look like brutal detachment on his part, but in those more innocent days such things were much harder to credit. Today over thirty countries are said to practise torture – imagine, thirty Gestapos.

Now, of course, I'm refining my pictures again, or (if you prefer it) decoding these messages from the past, a double decode in this case, trying to see through her eyes what I knew only at second-hand through his. She told him in fragments, in broken sentences and isolated pictures, from which certain images came through to him very vividly, like the horrid little cell and the lamp-lit room upstairs. She never even finished the story, but let it die away as she curled up close against him and finally slept. Outside in the dark the early cocks were crowing.

The big ginger cat is sitting beside me on the desk. When he was young he had terrible fights and came limping home with holes chewed in his flanks, so we had him neutered. He eats well and walks portly in his beautiful tawny coat. As I write this late at night the house is quiet except for an occasional passing car, with the radio playing *Cabaret*. He leaps smoothly on to the desk and looks slightly abashed as he lands on a sheet of manuscript and skids across the desk to a halt. Now he sits beside me, listening to the radio and dozing. He is getting old, his tongue sticks out and he dribbles sometimes when he sleeps, and late at night he sits close beside me for company. The old dog is asleep not far away, under the model-cabinet. They used to fight each other, but now they have an armed truce, and even sometimes sleep on the same couch. At night the dog sleeps outside the bedroom door. Old creatures want company. Even animals fear whatever is out there in the dark.

By the time Saul Scourby got to this point in the story, I was interested enough to want to hear the rest of it. Even though I didn't relish the thought of the journey home in the dark, I hoped that my captain would take his time in the Officers' Mess. Sure enough, when I went outside for a leak and to see what was happening there was a roar of chat from behind the blacked-out windows, the jangle of a piano and a bit of singing. The night was pretty quiet, with a low chilly ground-mist and a cold glow of artificial moonlight somewhere along the river, and the searchlights doing a slow pavane eastward over Germany.

Back in the dust-smelling gloom of the barn Saul had made another brew of tea and got one of the cooks to whip up some corned-beef sandwiches. We settled down again and he went on with the story.

Well, you wouldn't Adam-and-Eve it, because I always sleep pretty light, ready for trouble like, but next morning I slept in. I was dreaming about my granny and church on Sunday and church bells, and when I woke up the church down the road was clanking that dreary bell they had. Her side of the bed was empty, and it shook me a bit, because I thought she might have risked it and scarpered. First thing I reached out for my short knife and the sten, always laid ready to hand at night on the rush-bottomed chair by the bed, but they was both where I left them.

I could smell bacon frying and there was a clank as the oven door opened. So I pulled on my shirt and went into the kitchen, and there she was in her purple Japanesy wrap-thing with her red hair all loose, looking sleepy and warm. So I slips my hands round her and gives her a good hug, where she stood by the stove.

Outside, it was one of them summer mists like they had in Normandy – remember? (And I remembered the golden mist full of dissolved sunlight, the hedges powdered with dew and the fertile smell of summer, and I laid the memory of it alongside the cold creeping greyness outside the barn.) It looked sort of dodgy, you couldn't see more than about twenty yards, and it crossed my mind that someone might have clever ideas with a grenade or something. So I kept my eyes open all the way to the bog, and back again.

Then I went round into the wash-house, where the flagstones were still splashed and damp where she'd washed herself earlier. I stripped and soused a bucket of that cold water over myself, and it didn't half wake me up.

Well, she made me another good breakfast – your English breakfast, she called it – and she ate a bit with me. I suppose it was a change for her from that coffee and rolls they always have. It's poor food that. She enjoyed her bacon and sausage, and we chatted for a while.

I says to her, Why didn't you explain to someone, about the Gestapo and all that?

I tried to, she says, but who would believe? I had slept with Germans, that was enough.

I didn't say no more, after all I only had her word for the whole thing, didn't I?

Then I went outside to have a smoke while she

cleaned up. And for a while it was like old home week, the number of people there was passing along that stretch of road.

The mist was thinning. I could see old Wolf-face doing his turn at keeping look-out by the old beech tree. A kid came running up the road from the direction of the church, a little boy of maybe eight dressed in one of them blue smocks like they have, faded, scrubbed, and a black beret. He stops and has a good look at me.

Hullo, I says, friendly-like. You know what these kids are, they like the uniform and they trust soldiers, knowing we're a soft lot really, always thinking we'd like to have our own kids about us.

You English soldat? he says.

That's right, I says.

You give me cigarette? he says, cheeky.

I'll give you a thick ear, I says. How about some chocolate? (Because I had a bit in my pocket just in case.)

Oh, chocolate, he says as if it was gold-dust.

I give it to him, and he was nibbling at it when a woman came up the road. There was others behind her. They was coming back from church and the kid must've run on ahead.

The woman had on a black dress and a shawl over her head. She was thin and dark and you could see her in the boy, the resemblance. She's a bit anxious and clucks over the boy like a hen, but when she sees how he's enjoying the chocolate she smiles a bit, shy-like. Then she looks over my shoulder and her face changes.

I swung around because it might be trouble, but it was only Belle, in her blue-and-white dress, with her hair braided up, looking like a Sunday-school teacher. The woman, the mother, screamed out something and she caught the kid an open-handed slap that staggered him and sent the bit of chocolate flying into the dust. The poor kid began to holler and she grabbed his arm and dragged him up the road, giving him a proper piece of her mind.

I was going to go after her and make her let the kid alone when I heard voices behind and there was half-a-dozen more of them, oldish men and women mostly, all in Sunday black. One of them leaned over the gate and said something to Belle, but she stood her ground. I stood in the gateway and stared them down till they went off up the road, but still turning back to look at us. They stopped and had a proper palaver with Wolf-face and the others up the hill, but I took Belle by the arm and we went back inside.

Well, like I said, it was a bit of old home week, because the next thing that happened was that the Indestructible Yank dropped in again. Come to think of it, it could have been quite a bit later, because I went back to the front garden and stopped out there for a while, smoking and watching the last of the mist clear and the sun come through, and generally keeping an eye on things. The Mass-bell had stopped a while back, and instead I heard the Angelus what they rung at midday, dong-dong-dong and stop, dong-dong-dong and stop, like that. I see the Indestructible Yank strolling down the road, and there he was again, large as life, with that beefy close-shaven face and a uniform like it was just fresh from the laundry and a smell of perfume. He has a small pack slung over one shoulder, and he carries a tommy-gun, very heavy and shiny. He looks tough but sort of unreal, like a soldier doll.

Hi, he says.

Hullo, I says.

Say, fella, he says, I'm real sorry about yesterday. Didn't know you had interests here.

Well, I have, I says, short-like.

Aw, come on, he says, we've had that bit. I'm your friend, honest, I'm a real friendly guy.

He was looking past me, watching for Belle, but she didn't show though I reckoned she was sure to be watching, and he knew it too. I didn't make any move to stand out of the gateway. He slipped the small pack off his shoulder and put it down by the gatepost.

Look, he says, I brought you some stuff. C'mon, take it, we got plenty. It's real good, tinned turkey and stuff. You got enough to eat? This'll vary your diet. C'mon, share it with the strawberry blonde, with my compliments.

So I thought, why not? We could do with a change from all that bullybeef, and after all where's the harm? Of course he wants Belle to remember him as a good provider, generous. But he's wrong. That's what the Yanks never understand, they give people things and expect them to be grateful, and the people aren't grateful because they think the Yanks have got all this stuff and they just can't help giving some of it away, anyhow.

Me, I took it and thanked him nicely, because food's food at any time. He ambled off up the road again with that gun slung over his shoulder.

I took the pack inside and emptied it out on to the kitchen table. Belle watched – sure enough, she'd been watching from behind the curtains. It was good stuff like he said, a big tin of turkey and another one of fruit salad, and coffee and even a tinned cake, all just like Christmas. American fags too, Camels. She was still angry, but I think the fags helped, because she'd told me she liked them better than English ones.

Look, I says, we can use this stuff, and the Yanks aren't all that bad. It's just that they aren't really good at being soldiers. They're only playing at it, so they have to have lots of stuff to keep them happy. Not like us, we're used to not having much.

(I think Saul was right about this. Each country has a character of its own that comes out in its army. The Germans fought like engineers, the Russians like peasants, the Americans like movie cowboys, the British like workmen, grumbling, doing their job and taking their pay. An army of mercenaries indeed –

they're the ones to be careful of, the tradesmen.)

Then she told me some of the things that the Jerries had said about the Yanks in their propaganda. She said that it was the Yanks they really picked on, how corrupt they were and decadent and all that. They didn't seem to mind the British so much, though they seemed frightened of the Jocks.

It didn't surprise me none, and I told her the old one about the Jerry on the radio – you know – Ven der Britisch Schpitfeuer come ofer, ve duck – ven der Cherman Messerschmitt come ofer, you duck – ven der Americanisch Lightning come ofer, ve both duck.

That made her laugh, and it didn't help the Yank any. You see, he still hadn't understood. He meant the turkey and stuff as a present, but to her it was like showing that he'd still got his claim in. Like a down payment on a haitch-pee, with her as the property. She was still against him – that was all right, but I didn't want her sulky with me. I looked out of the window and the mist was quite gone and it was a real sunny day.

Cheer up, girl, I says, how about a picnic?

She looks up and says, We cannot go far.

No need to, I says, there's a good spot right out there at the back in your orchard.

We spread out the tins on the table and began to open them. The turkey looked all right, all white meat and jelly, very savoury. He'd even put in a little tin of cranberry sauce, the way the Yanks like it. There was mixed vegetables, biscuits and butter, cheese, some real coffee. We got it all ready and I picked out the spot in the orchard.

The grass had grown long all over, except in one part, a kind of square patch overhung by four very old trees. There was a lot of moss there, perhaps on purpose to keep an open space, perhaps just because it was an old part of the orchard. I laid a blanket there and a white cloth she brought out. When we put out the food it made a real good spread. I had my sten and the other tools laid handy, but I didn't really expect trouble, we was so well hidden on all sides, so still and quiet.

I looked it over and I says, joking like, Pity we ain't got no champagne.

Wait, she says, and she runs off through the orchard towards the wash-house. Soon she comes back with two bottles and there was dried earth on them and the little metal plates were all rusty so that they broke up.

Quite a lot of it was buried, she says, and the Boches have not found it all.

She showed me how to ease out the cork and when I poured it out it had a pretty good head on it, in the tumblers. It was the stuff all right, and it went down nicely with that turkey. We sat there on the grass talking and eating. It was really warm there and still under the trees. I was in shirt-sleeve order but presently I took my shirt off so as to get the sun, while she loosened her blouse and unbound that beautiful red hair so that it rippled down over her shoulders. We finished the turkey and the bottle about the same time, and I lay back and stared up at the sky through the branches hung thick with little half-ripe apples. She moved over so she was sitting close beside me, looking down at me. I felt warm and peaceful and sort of innocent.

She'd been talking about Paris and the painters and art and all that – I couldn't follow all of it. She looks at me and says, There is a marvellous painting by Manet, I feel like it now, it is called *The Lunch on the Grass*. There are two men and two girls, you know, having a picnic very like this. Only the men are dressed in the costume of gentlemen, trousers, waistcoats, everything. One of the girls is quite nude. They are like classic nymphs in Arcadie, you know? You do not know, do you, you stupid big Englishman?

But when she said it she bent down and kissed me, very sweetly.

I'm not much on art, I says, but it sounds all right.

All right, she says, all right, is that all you can say? It is superb, a vision. I should like to be like that, an Arcadian.

What, sitting on the grass with no clothes on?

Yes, she says.

Dare you, I says, joking.

Here, she says, open the other bottle, the way I showed you.

Now, it took a bit of doing, breaking off the rusty wire and easing out the old cork and pouring it all nice and creamy into the tumblers. While I did it she stood up and moved away behind me and came back. Then I looked up and it really took my breath away. She'd slipped all her clothes off – I don't think she had much on anyway – and she was standing there with the sunlight dappling down on her, with her red hair all loose and golden about her face, and her beautiful big charlies and the tawny hair at her crotch and her long white legs. For a second she just stood there, then she eased down beside me, sitting with her legs tucked under her. She took up her glass and drank it off in little quick sips, to steady herself like.

You really are a smasher, I says. You really are. I never seen nothing like you. I'll remember this all my days.

She looks at me, pleased, and sort of giggles.

Now you, she says.

I thought you said the gentlemen had waistcoats and trousers and all? I says.

Oh, that is in the picture, she says, we can do better. And she kissed me very lightly and reached over and began to tug at my belt.

Here, hold on, I says, but I just couldn't help it, with her half-helping and half-hindering, I got out of my trousers and soon I was sitting there mother-naked beside her.

Now it really is like the garden of Eden, I says, and we drank on it and refilled our glasses, but I wasn't sure.

Because she looked down at me and saw how I was

and she says, Is there something wrong? What is wrong, Saul? Is it my fault?

No, I says, it's hard to say, Belle, but – it's like I'm a night man, see? I never taken a woman in daylight, see? not to look upon her nakedness. And I never had a red-haired woman before you, I says, and like this it makes me feel strange and it puts me down.

Lie down, she says, putting her hand on my shoulder.

No, I says, but the wine was strong in me and I lay back with soft grass under me. She leaned over me and she laughed in her throat and she says, I can see the apple trees reflected in your eyes.

Then she bent closer and I says, And I can see myself reflected in yours.

Then she bent right down and kissed me, her red hair hung all around my face and it smelt like ripe apples. She set herself astride of me and she says, Is it so?

And I says, No, and then, Yes.

Is it not right? she says.

And I says, Everything's right.

And so it was, after all, the best I ever had.

When it was quite finished she rolled off me and lay there in the grass with her eyes shut. It was my turn to lean over her.

Was it all right? I says.

And she smiles all rosy and says, It was all right.

Was it like the picture?

It was like the picture.

You're an artist, I says. If loving was an art, you'd be

in the National Gallery in London. I've been there once, I says. I didn't like her thinking I was ignorant.

I eased down beside her. The sun was off the orchard now, but it was still very warm and still there under the trees.

There is a poem also, she says, by Baudelaire. And she went on saying the words in French, something about order and beauty looks calm – she began to tell me what it said, it seemed to mean a lot to her. What with the warmth and stillness and her so close I must have fallen asleep.

But we know what the poem was. It was Baudelaire's *Invitation to the Voyage*. I have it in front of me now, in the old edition of *Flowers of Evil*, published by Editions Verda, 11 Cité Dupetit-Thouars, Paris, and sold for twelve (old) francs. When did she give it to him? He couldn't read it, so he gave it to me. It has her signature in it, 'Isabelle Pradier', in a careful unformed hand, in violet ink. The cheap pages have turned brown, and it falls open of itself at page 105, '*L'Invitation au Voyage*', as if the pages had been turned by the ghost of a hand. The dead poet begins to speak to the dead woman –

> *Mon enfant, ma soeur,*
> *Songe à la douceur*
> *D'aller là-bas vivre ensemble! . . .*

My child, my sister, dream of the sweetness of going down there and living together! To love easily, to love and die, in this country which is so much like you! The hazy suns in its smudged skies have a mysterious magic for me, like those treacherous eyes of yours, smiling through tears.

> *Là, tout n'est qu'ordre et beauté,*
> *luxe, calme et volupté.*

There it is all order, beauty, luxury, peace, pleasure.

And he goes on to tell her how they will live in the old house with its dark lustrous furniture, its deep mirrors. Outside, canal-boats sleep at their moorings. Setting suns clothe the fields and streets in daffodil and gold. The world sleeps in warm light. It is all order, beauty, luxury, peace, pleasure.

She must have learned that poem at school and loved it and remembered it somehow behind the loveless couplings and the terror and the despair. She dreamed of that order and beauty and found it perhaps in the lush summer orchard.

Well (said Saul) what woke me up was a fly settling on my face. A hand gently brushed it away. The orchard was in shadow now and a mite chilly, so she'd tucked the blanket around me. And the flies had found us, perhaps from the dead cows over in the field, and so there she was with her dress loose about her, sitting beside me on the grass waving the flies away so that I should have my sleep. When she saw me awake, she kissed me and went off into the house, leaving me to get my clothes and gear together.

I went into the house from the back, through the wash-house. The cottage was empty, but this time I didn't think of her scarpering on me, and sure enough I could see that up the garden the door of the jakes was closed. I stood there smoking and looking out in the garden. Big Stupid was on duty up the hill, and the sky was all bright and smoky.

A jeep came bumping down the road, trailing a dust cloud. At first I thought I might just pull back and quietly fade, but it drew up with a jolt at the gate and out hopped our Lieutenant Mortimer, large as life. I reckoned that he was looking for me and that Charlie must have told him about me and where I was. So I straightened myself up and slipped on my jacket, and when I met him by the gate I chucked him up a smart salute. He had a purring lah-di-dah voice, sort of put on, but he wasn't a bad officer at all. He didn't know a lot but he knew how to take advice, and he swore like a bastard when we took casualties.

Aha, Corporal Scourby, he says, I thought I'd find you here. And how's your passionate weekend, eh?

Bit of all right, sir, I says.

Well, I wish it was me, he says. Never mind, I'm liaising with Div and there's a nurse I know up there, if she isn't already bespoke.

Good luck, sir, I says, and I suppose I meant it.

I could see he was smartened up, and he was carrying his swaggerstick, tapping it against his glove, like he was impatient and embarrassed. Behind him, his driver –

bloke named Carnall, would you believe it – kept idling and revving his engine as if he wanted to be off.

Corporal, says Lieutenant Mortimer, Private Smith (that was Charlie) told me about your problem. I asked a friend in Mil Guv and I'm afraid it's no good. Once we start moving we'll rely on the Resistance for a lot of intelligence and flank protection. We can't afford to antagonize them, and they're very prickly. So instructions are not to upset them in any way. The woman's their problem. We can't do a thing. I'm sorry if that's bad news.

It is that, sir, I says. (As a matter of fact I hadn't expected this, it was good of old Charlie to try – like I said, he was stuck on Belle in his own way.) But it's not a surprise. Thanks for trying, sir.

Think nothing of it, he says. Well, I'm not here.

He touched his cap-brim with his swaggerstick, and he was off.

The door of the bog creaked open. Belle came cautiously up the path. She must have been waiting for him to leave.

Was that your officer? she says. What did he say?

I put my arm about her shoulders and led her inside.

It's good news, I says. Good old Charlie told him about you, so he called some friends he has in Military Government. They were pretty important friends, and they talked to the local command of the Resistance. And that did the trick – they'll be ordered off, them up the hill, and told to leave you alone.

She was staring up into my face all the time I was shooting her this line, wondering what she ought to believe. I must have made it sound all right, because when I finished, it was as if she just let go. She smiled and rested her head on my shoulder, and she says, Perhaps I am going to live, in spite of all.

You better Adam-and-Eve it, I says.

And I wished I could myself.

What followed after this was, in a way, the obscurest part of the story, mainly because there was little of it that he could put into his kind of words. He could only say banal things like, We sat and watched the sunset, or, I never seen her so happy, or, We would sit and play pontoon. Again he slipped into this way of talking as if life with the woman had gone on for a long time, and in a way it had.

They'd reached a state of quiet and contentment, like a long-married couple. They lived as if this evening was just one of a chain of thousands, stretching before and after. (In any stable relationship, we stand as it were between the two mirrors of past and future and seeing our days receding, multiplied to infinity in either direction. In Luc Peire's *Environment Three*, it's a room with the floor and ceiling made of mirrors. Up isn't really so impressive – we're used to looking up into the emptiness of space, at night when the sky has rolled away. But looking down into empty space and an infinite regress of your own reflection – that's disturbing. The room becomes a lift, sinking down through endless selves, a time-lift in free fall. Entropy. Free fall. Entropy is free-falling in time.) They created for themselves a temporary past and future. Or, you might say, they expanded that evening into the life-time of a marriage or a liaison. So what happened went perhaps like this:

The champagne in the orchard would have left him thirsty, so he got her to put the kettle on the hob – she'd already stirred up the fire in the grate – and make some tea from the ration-pack, the powdered tea, milk and sugar stirred in together to make a good warm brew. While she stared into the grate and waited for the kettle to boil, he went through into the wash-house at the back and washed out a set of smalls. He had to bring them back through the kitchen so that he could hang them in a corner of the garden that caught the late sun, and she exclaimed at him for not leaving this woman's work to her.

He'd rather counted on this, and after they'd had their tea, sitting together at the old scrubbed table, he brought her a sock that needed a good piece of darning. She also remembered and asked him for his battle-dress jacket, which needed a button or two tightening and one of his corporal's stripes resewn where it had caught and torn. Actually he was very capable and handy, as you might have guessed, at all that kind of work, but it was pleasant to be sitting there with his feet under the table while the woman bent over her work, stitching neatly with the khaki jacket draped across her lap.

Of course, when I say that he had his feet under the table, I'm using the customary army metaphor, meaning that he was at home there, received as a guest, domesticated, probably sleeping with the woman. It said a lot for the British soldier's idea of homely sexual joys. As the proverb went later in occupied Germany: in the Russian zone the typical sex-crime is rape; in the American, prostitution; in the British, bigamy. There's a lot of truth in that.

Actually he was sitting on the sill of the open doorway with his back against the door-jamb and his half-empty mug of tea beside him. He had his sten and his cleaning gear out, going through his daily routine of cleaning and lightly oiling. Piercingly there came into his mind the picture of himself as a boy of six or seven, sitting in the doorway of his granny's cottage, spooning out of a chipped blue bowl his bread-and-milk well sweetened with brown sugar. Beside the kitchen table, the old lady was knitting at a long piece that was to be his winter scarf. As her busy needles went in sliding quickly over and under, she looked down at him watchfully over her low spectacles.

He set aside the sten and its magazines and began carefully to hone his two knives, spitting on the bit of whetstone he always carried with him for the purpose. The rasp of steel on stone pleased him, and he repeated it slowly, deliberately. It was her silence that stopped him, as he became aware that her quiet movements had ceased. He looked up and found her staring, not at him, but at the sharp tool lying against the stone.

Do you use that, she said, to fight? Is it to kill?

Sometimes I do, he said matter-of-factly, sometimes killing has to be done.

Does it hurt them? she asked in the same flat voice.

Not so you'd notice, he said, at least, they go quick and quiet. That's the whole idea. At least, mostly they do. It's only when I miss my stroke that it gets a bit nasty. But I don't like that to happen, and it seldom does.

She finished her work on the jacket before holding it up for a final inspection and putting it aside on the table. She came down and sat beside him on the step.

What is it like to kill a man? she asked.

He handed her a cigarette and lit it, and one for himself.

Like fucking a woman, he said, after the first one they're all the same.

Oh, you are horrible, she said, jumping to her feet in sudden passion. Completely horrible. Truly English. A brute, to kill men and to – yes – fuck women.

He smiled at her his hard lonely smile.

Don't take on so, love, he said, I was only joking.

I do not like such jokes, she said, still standing up, and turned stiffly away from him.

Come on, he said, I didn't mean it.

I gave you good love, she said, all I could.

I know. The best.

And you say this now to me?

I didn't mean it, he said. Look, I enjoy going with girls. They're all beautiful, all loving, all different. Killing's another matter. You don't want to have feelings about it – either liking it or being upset. It's like a job to be done. The less feelings you have, the better it's done, the quicker it's done. Now sit down like a good girl, and I'll tell you a story.

It was once early in the war when I was on patrol with a sergeant name of Berry – Harry Berry. He was a short fat bloke – at least, that's what he looked like, with a sort of moon-face, but really he was very quick and crafty. But not very nice.

Well, we had a scratch platoon for this job, and we pushed on to a place where there was a house with a German strong-point inside. You know how quiet it was between the lines, with no one sure where the other side was, not even on the map. I liked it that way, it gave you more of a free hand, and you were pretty safe from bumping into anything real big.

Do you want me to tell you this? he asked.

Yes, she said, go on.

And she sat close beside him on the step, watching him, as if she was trying to understand something.

So we come up close to this house, well hidden near some trees. And everything was quiet, except for those Jerries, there was some of them talking, just loud

enough to hear. Now, this might have been part of a
defence line, or just a strong-point on its own. So me
and old Perry we decided to work around the back, if
we could, and see what we could see. We shouldn't
really have done that, being two NCOs, because it
meant leaving the platoon with only a young lance-
jack in charge. But we was pretty sure of ourselves, too
sure perhaps, like you'll see.

We worked round behind the house all right, no
trouble, and couldn't find a thing. There was a sort of
sunken lane there with trees overhanging it, and I
thought I should cross it to get just a closer shooftee
from the other side. I signed to Berry to wait, and I
went down into the lane very quietly. Lucky for me,
because when I stood there and got my head up I
saw there was a Jerry there. I couldn't make out for a
second what he was doing, because he just stood there
and seemed to be staring at the sky. Then – I could have
laughed – I saw he was having a jimmy-riddle, standing
there with his gun slung and his other weapon un-
slung, if you follow me.

I thought for a second. It seemed a shame to take a
man like that, just easing himself, but he might have
turned his head at any minute, or I might have trod
on a twig. So I decided to play it safe and take him. I
had my knife out and I was nearly on his back when
my feet slipped out from under me. I should have
said that there had been rain earlier, and the clay in
the lane was damp and greasy.

Well, there I was flat on my arse and my knife gone

flying. The Jerry was pretty scared, you can imagine, but he was a quick man, and he had his gun coming up and his mouth open to shout. I thought it was my lot, I really did.

Then standing there behind him was Harry Berry. I still don't know how he did it, but he came out of the dark behind the Jerry, just like magic. And in the same move he had his arm hooked round the Jerry's throat with his elbow under the chin, and when he levered I could hear the Jerry's neckbone crack.

She was looking at him as he told her this, with her face very set, and she winced when he said that he could hear the Jerry's neckbone crack. So he put his hand over hers where it rested on the step, and went on.

That's what I mean about not feeling, he said. I stopped to feel sorry for that Jerry and he nearly had me – if he'd warned the others, they might have wiped out the whole platoon. Berry saved me, much as I disliked him, and I think he knew it.

We didn't say a dickybird to each other, but we cleaned out the Jerry's pockets, which gave us some useful stuff to take back – he was a sergeant and he'd got a movement order and some other things on him. But the funny thing was what Berry told me when we got back. We went back the same way we come, as quick and quiet as we could. We reported in and went off to the cookhouse to get ourselves some supper. And I thanked Sergeant Harry Berry for what he done, as was proper. Then, Forget it, he says, you'd have done the same. Besides, I like that. D'you know – and he gave a sort of giggle – when I took him, it excited me, and I come in my pants, just like in a woman.

That's what he said to me, just like that. After that, I disliked him more than ever, even though he'd saved my life. I didn't want to be like him, I didn't want to enjoy it. He was a dirty bastard. Besides, that's another way of having feelings about it, wasn't it? So I managed not to go out on patrol with him again. Sure enough, he got himself killed a bit later, he wanted it too much, took a chance, I suppose.

She shivered beside him and looked up at the sky. The long dusk was drawing to a close. (Do you remember them sunsets in Normandy, Bom? said Corporal Scourby. You know, when the roads began to dry out and the dust hung in the air. All red and gold, they was.) So she shivered and looked up at the sky hung with red and gold; so he slipped his right arm round her and drew her close. With his left hand, that large rough clever hand, he took her left hand, all soft and ringless.

When will it end, the war? she said.

Soon, he said, soon. P'raps even this year, couple of months even. Once we get going, and them Russians, it can't be long, not now.

She shook her head doubtfully.

It has been so long, she said, we have forgotten to hope.

Don't give up, girl, he said. Just think, one day you'll

be an old lady telling your grandchildren all about this.

She obstinately would not be comforted.

It is not true, she said, not for me. Where can I go? What can I do?

I'll tell you what you can do, he said. I'll come back as soon as the war's over and I can get leave, and we'll marry. We'll go back and live in England, and no one need know.

(And perhaps as he said this he meant it, for perhaps he needed some comforting dreams too. It was the start of a kind of game between them, to play house, as if they were old married people and this was how they lived, had lived, would live, might live, grow old, have children. Desperately she joined in the game.)

Come in, she said, it is cold. Let this be our house. Come into our house.

So they went in; she drew the curtains and lit a candle while he livened up the fire with a knob of wood and a bit of kindling. There was a pack of old greasy cards on the mantelpiece. He took them down and laid out a game of patience on the table. The one candle was not enough, so he reached out to the top shelf of the kitchen dresser, where two candles in brass candlesticks stood on each side of a dark wooden crucifix.

Please do not touch that, she said quickly, look in the drawer, there is another candle there.

Why not, he said. They're good candles, not used.

They are blessed candles, she said, for the dead. When a person lies dead in the house, one places the crucifix at the head, the candles on each side. It is the custom.

She went over to the stove and began to make their supper. For a time there was a companionable silence, broken only by her quiet movements at stove and sinkboard, the scrape of the casserole being moved on the stove, the rattle as she opened the grate and pushed in more wood, the tinkle of a spoon in a bowl. The cards clicked as he laid them on the table. He played fairly and with concentration, turning the cards in rigid sequence. When the game refused to come out, he neatly gathered the cards, shirred them together and began again. The first card up in the left-hand column was the Queen of Spades: he frowned over it.

Pique dame, she said, nodding towards it.

She was standing behind him watching the game, with her left hand laid lightly on his shoulder.

They say she brings misfortune, she said.

Who says so?

Oh – old women.

Our old women say the same. (A death in the family, his granny used to say, but he was careful not to quote that.) Me, I think it's a load of cobblers. You know, like teacups and horoscopes and all that bollocks. Look, there's the Queen of Hearts, that could be you, couldn't it? and here comes the

Knave of Spades to cover her, like it might be me?

He grinned slyly up at her, but her face in the shifting candlelight was shadowy and unsmiling.

You know what that means? she asked. It is really swords – the Spanish say *espada*, a sword. He is the swordsman. Like you.

She touched her fingertips to the knife in its sheath at his belt. He tensed up and pushed her hand away.

Don't do that, girl, he said sharply.

Why not?

I don't like it, that's all. I don't want it touched, that's all.

(And he couldn't explain this, because it was a kind of primitive *tapu* thing. This was a man's weapon, and if a woman touched it the fighting magic might somehow leak away. In some ways he was very atavistic; as I've suggested before, he was an instinctive hunter and warrior, and this feeling of power in his weapons, part magical, part practical, part phallic, was an unthinking part of his special abilities. Without it, his skill would be diminished, perhaps disastrously.)

Then she brought the supper to the table, and it was first a vegetable soup made up of scraps but tasty, and then bullybeef made over into a kind of meat-loaf with herb sauce and little dumplings manufactured out of tinned potatoes.

You're a great cook, you know, he said.

I know, she said.

When you come to England, he said carefully, you'll be able to cook all you want.

Thank you, she said mockingly, but I wish to come as your wife, not your cook.

Don't mistake me, girl, I mean there's plenty of good food there. But it's like my grandad used to say, God sends the food and the Devil sends cooks. He liked rabbit-pie, did my grandad, and fat bacon, and he lived to be eighty or more.

Food was bad in England in the war? she asked.

Oh, we ate enough, he said, but never too much, and some of it was poor stuff, it still is.

So with us, she said. And the *marché noir*, the black market?

So with us, he mocked gently.

He poured rum and water into the glasses, and they ate and drank in silence. Abruptly –

How many children shall we have? she asked.

Three, he said promptly. A boy and a girl and a boy. Only I bet the girl will be a wicked little red-headed bitch like you. I'll have to watch her.

She nodded at him eagerly.

You will watch me too?

Like a hawk, he said. Like a hawk sitting in the air over a rabbit-warren.

And if I am wicked?

He touched his knife and grinned his hard grin.

I wouldn't lay a finger on you, girl. But the bloke, he better watch out, otherwise I'll have his balls for breakfast. Fried, with bacon.

You are a horrible Englishman and I love you, she said as she bent over him and kissed him hard. Now I go to have a bath.

Don't spend too long in that luxurious tub, he said.

She took the stub of candle and went out to the wash-house, carrying the kettle with her. He heard the hot water poured into a bucket, and the pleasant sound of cold water being dipped from the water-butt, and the splashing as she washed herself down. She had left the door open, so that by shifting his head slightly he could watch her long shadow moving on the wall in the wavering guttering light of the candle.

He turned back to stare into the fire, smoking and thinking his own thoughts.

When she came back she was naked under the old purple dressing-gown, with her hair loose and dark and damp about her shoulders. She too sat close to the fire, towelling and combing her hair till the rich brightness came back to it. He watched her possessively, appreciatively. In the firelight slowly dying in the open grate she was all pink and rosy, one shoulder exposed by the loose dressing-gown, scrubbed innocent face, hair shining like a copper kettle.

Now, she said, you have a wife and children, so how will you make a trade?

I might sign on for the regular army, he said. It's not a bad life, not in peacetime, and I reckon I could make sergeant.

She looked at him slyly.

You would be away very often, she said. I should be unfaithful to you.

Then I tell you what we'll do. We'll move out of the country into some town like Blandford or Dorchester. I'll have a gratuity and I've got a little money put by what came from my gran. We'd buy a little tobacconist and newsagent's – I reckon I could do well with that. Or maybe we could get into Swanage or Poole, where there's a good summer season with holiday crowds. In peacetime that is. But we'd move out of the country into some town.

She continued to stare into the fire.

We should be old, she said, some day we should be old.

And after they'd talked some more the big black kettle began to rattle again. He took it and the stub of candle and went out for his wash-down. She was still staring at the dull fire when he came back, with a towel wrapped round his middle.

We've been married so long, she said.

Years.

She reached out for his hand and led him towards the bedroom, the purple dressing-gown trailing behind her on to the floor. She pulled back the worn patchwork quilt and the mended sheets and lay down on the bed. He went into her without words or play, yet holding her close and tenderly, and when he came it was so gentle that there hardly seemed to be a climax, just a dying away.

Afterwards he rested on his back, staring up into the half-dusk of the summer night. She lay close to him, her head on his shoulder, her loose hair still smelling of the garden and of fresh pump-water.

She laid hold of his free hand and drew it against her soft belly.

Perhaps we shall have a baby, she said.

Be good, wouldn't it? he said. It'd be good.

I feel it, you know. I feel it here, now. I can tell.

Not so soon, you can't. It's just a feeling.

No, I know it.

All right, if you say so, girl. Anyway it wouldn't hardly be surprising, would it?

She laughed softly and hid her face against his shoulder.

I do believe you're blushing, he teased her. I do believe you're shamed of what you done.

She lifted her head and looked up at him. Outside in the night sky a flight of German fighter-bombers came in low with pulsing engines and roared away towards the beach-heads and the shipping in the bay.

Not shamed, she said, I am a happy woman. But you make me to feel – *tu me fais timide*. I am timid to you?

I wouldn't say that, he said. No, that's not the word. You're not scared of me are you, girl?

Not scared. *Timide*.

You're shy with me, he guessed.

Yes, shy, now. I feel like a young girl.

Well, you're not all that old, are you?

That is not what I mean.

We'll have a lot of things to explain to each other, he said.

He brought his hand up to her hair, bunching it, feeling its weight and thickness, while he waited for the roar of another flight of German planes to die away. Then he felt the words forced out of him and he said:

You know, I'm the one that's been shy, with you. It's funny and I don't quite know why. Years ago, though, there was something, it sort of stayed on my mind. This girl, she wasn't my first, but she was the first I went with regular, and she was very loving but very modest. Thatcher's daughter she was, name of Milly. Leastwise, her old man had been a thatcher, but it was a dying trade, and he earned a crust at odd jobs, like hedging and ditching, though most of the money went in the boozer. My grandad knew him well, used to call on him when he needed an extra hand. That's how I knew him, then his daughter. We used to meet at night, we'd walk across the fields between our homes, and there was an old hay-barn only half-used, a good place to meet, and quiet. True, there was a farmer's watch-dog thereabouts, but I could always make a dog be quiet, it's all in knowing how to speak to them.

Now, like I said, she was very modest, and she'd never undress, no matter how much I teased her. She'd just lift her clothes, and we'd go to it there in the dry-smelling hay.

How her old man found out I don't know, but find

out he did. Maybe someone in the village night-wandered like me and spotted us, and told him. I should have explained that he was a sour-tempered man, what with him rather coming down in the world and then losing his wife sudden-like, and having too much liking for the drink, though some said that that had come later. And when he found out about her he took a rope's end to her and called her all manner of foul names, so loud you could hear him t'other end of the village.

She was a quiet girl, timid-like, and after that she dursn't come near me. Only sent a message through another girl to ask my forgiveness. After that she just moped, stayed home and waited on her father, and moped.

Well, one night, it was autumn and turning sharp, he came banging on our door at eleven at night, with us all in bed. So my grandad hollers out to him to know who it is, and what he wants.

It's Milly, he says and he sounds very strong in drink. It's my Milly. I know she's run off with your bastard grandson, and you got her there now.

You're wrong, says Grandad, but hold on.

He pulled on his shirt and trousers and went to the door. T'other man, Milly's father, he come in raging and wanted to go for me. If he had I might have killed him and swung, for I'd been told what he'd done to Milly with the rope's end. But my Grandad stood up to him, I can still see him standing there in his old flannel shirt and moleskin trousers with his braces hanging down, and the big man glaring down at him and raging, like a great raging bull bailed up by a little old bandy bull-terrier.

She's not here, says Grandad, and she's not been here. And the way you treat her she'll have run away, I reckon, and who's to blame her?

So the big man tried to push into the house, but whichever way he turned Grandad was before him, like the terrier at the bull's nose, until he'd quite faced him down.

After a while the other man turned crying drunk, and began to sob and carry on about his only daughter, and what a good girl she'd been before this, and what a comfort she'd been when his dear wife passed on. It began to look like he really was in trouble and wanted to search for her, so my Grandad agreed to help. I went too, I didn't really want to, but my Granny made me, to keep the peace, she said.

We couldn't do much that night. When we told the constable, he didn't take it too serious, knowing how the old man treated her, he thought she'd run off. We had a look around, and got out early in the morning to knock on doors – no sign of her.

By evening the village started to take it serious, and the second day they made up search-parties. When nothing turned up, the excitement died away, though the police circulated her description, and everyone reckoned she'd made off to some town.

It was over a week when some boys who'd gone to the river to fish spotted something among the brambles. Being curious like boys are, they fished it out and it was a bundle of clothes, her clothes, rolled up tight and flung away into the bushes. They took it straight to the constable.

Then a boat was got and grappling hooks, and it was soon over. The body hadn't gone far, and on the third try they raised it. I was there, all the village was there. I saw it come up in the late afternoon sun, all swollen and slimy. That's the only time in my life I went and threw up. It was so strange, you see, she'd been so still and modest with me, would hardly lift her clothes. But she went naked into the river.

Pauvre vieux, she murmured against his cheek, *pauvre p'tit soldat*.

Her voice was blurred, close to sleep. He shifted slightly to make them both more comfortable and as he did so he felt her body relax itself completely as she slept.

He lay there for some time staring up into the dark, and I know no more than you do what was going through his mind at that point. I see him clearly enough, as he lies there in the faint reflected sky-shine of a summer night, his left arm beneath her shoulders as she lies half-turned towards him, his right arm bent up, supporting his head. The sheet and the faded coverlet have been carelessly drawn up, leaving bare his wide flat-muscled chest and the curve of her arm across it. Her hair spills down opulently upon his body and her. He turns his face slightly to check on his sten gun and short knife laid handy on the rush-bottomed chair beside the bed, and his eyes seem to glisten in the dark like a hunting animal's. Then he stares up again, reckoning over the sounds of the night, distant planes, lazy gunfire, ours, theirs. He lowers his free arm on to the coverlet. Calmly, lightly, he falls asleep.

What is he thinking? He knows there is no help, but he has entered so whole-heartedly into the fantasy of domestic life and contentment which has been played out to comfort the woman that he almost believes it, wants it. For the first time in his hard, self-sufficient life he wants something for another. Tenderness begins to grow in him like green fern chance-dropped by birds on a rocky slope. Yet his face in sleep has its old sardonic look, his hand twitches on the coverlet, he moves his head from side to side and murmurs in his throat.

I held this double image of him in my mind – him there smoking and looking down at the hot blue glow of the burner, him in the imagined past, doubly screened from me by time and sleep. I held it there while he politely topped up my mug before going out for a leak.

When he came back into the barn he said, Getting quiet up at the mess, I reckon your bloke'll be moving pretty soon now. You want to hear the rest of this, or you had enough of it?

Tell me how it finished, I said, I've got to know that now.

Sure you're not bored, Bom?

No fear, I said, I can't wait. (But all the time I had a foreboding about how it was going to end.)

Well, said Saul, I woke up with the sun still pretty low in the sky, and I decided I'd better get cracking. So I roused up Belle and she was sleeping sound. I says to her, Time I was going, girl, but no worrying, mind, because we got it all fixed up.

All she says is, I will get you your breakfast.

She got naked out of the bed and pulled on her old purple wrap. I watched her as she walked out of the bedroom, with the wrap half off her shoulders, yawning and brushing her hair back with one hand. Soon I could hear her rattling about in the kitchen, drawing the grate.

We shall need some more wood very soon, she says.

I'll get some, I says, I'll bring you in a good pile before I go off.

I shall need some now, for the breakfast, she calls.

Right, I says.

Now, I didn't want to waste a lot of time at this stage, so I slipped on my trousers and I went quickly round the back where I'd left the wood ready chopped. Not much mist about today, but low cloud. The early Spitfires seemed pretty busy and there was a local barrage going in over on the left. I hauled in a big armful of wood and dropped it with a crash in the wood-box. It startled her where she stood there in a brown study. She turned round with a sort of troubled look.

Saul, she says, Saul, tell me again, will it be all right?

Belle, I says, Belle – supposing – would they really harm you?

Yes.

How d'you know?

I shouldn't have said it really, because I wasn't sure. Something made me want to know. She was close to the edge, it was as if her face broke up, she sat down in a chair.

Bon dieu, she says (again I'm helping out Saul's French), oh yes, there was another woman, they say she had – *on dit qu'elle avait chanté* –

Then she lost her English, like she did when she was moved or frightened – in bed sometimes too, when she had her climax. *Ils l'ont violée, puis crevé les yeux, enfin fusillée à la mitraillette.* And although the foreign words were too slurred to follow, there was no mistaking the pantomime that went with them. She mimed with little fierce gestures, clenched fist thrust at crotch, thumbs stabbing at eyes, the ritual gesture of traversing a Schmeisser. Rrrrudududuh. A kid's game gone bad.

I'd made a mistake (went on Saul) so I took her quick into my arms and kissed her.

Don't worry, sweetheart, they shan't touch you, I says, and I put up my hand and touched that marvellous red-gold hair. They shan't touch a hair of your head, I says, because even the hairs of thy head are numbered.

I'd seen to it that the water-barrel in the wash-house was topped up and the buckets were full. I stripped off and went in there with just a towel around me. The sun had begun to creep out and I unlatched the top half of the dutch door and set it wide open so as to let a bit of light in.

Then I called out to Belle.

Belle, I says, excited-like, come here quick.

What is it? she says.

Come and see, I says, I told you we'd be all right.

So she came hurrying in with her wrap still loose about her.

Look there, I says, and I set her so that she was looking out of the half-door across the garden.

Where? she says.

I put my arms around her and slipped her wrap down, leaving her bare. I slipped my left hand and arm under those beautiful charlies and gave them a last loving squeeze. She made a surprised sound, pleased too, and twisted her head back to kiss me. With my right hand I loosed the towel and reached for the long knife which I'd strapped to my thigh, under the towel.

At the last minute she must have sensed it. Her eyes went wide and wild like a frightened horse that smells death in a knacker's yard, but she pressed back close against me and clenched her mouth against mine like an iron gag. Then I went down and in with the long knife behind the collar-bone. I loosed my left arm, she groaned and fell on the cold flagged floor and began to kick and scrabble like an old dog dying in the road, but I knew that it was as good as over.

I knelt beside her and took her hand in mine while she died to comfort her, like, if she could still feel anything, but I don't think they can, not at that stage. Then I got to work with the buckets and the barrel and sluiced all down. I washed the blood off me and off her and watched it run all pale pink and gurgling down the drain-hole in the centre.

In the bedroom the big bed was still all rumpled up just as we'd got out of it, and when I felt it it was still warm from our bodies. That gave me a queer feeling, I can tell you. I stripped the bed off and laid it with a clean sheet from the linen-press. There was a big fluffy towel there too, which I took to dry her and wrap her in as I carried her back to the bedroom and laid her in the bed. But there was still some blood and water on her, which stained the clean sheet like a girl had lost her maidenhead on it.

So I laid her on the floor and pulled off the sheet, because I wanted everything done proper for her. I put a second sheet on the bed and laid her on it, covering the wound in her throat with a clean folded hankie.

Now I needed another sheet to cover her with. There wasn't one and this vexed me, until I found a fine old damask tablecloth, worn but good, so I laid that over her and covered her up to the chin. I smoothed out her long red hair, all dark from the water, and I closed her eyes. Then I took down the crucifix and the candles from the dresser where they'd been put against the time came for someone to die. I put the crucifix on the little shelf above the bed, and I arranged the two candles in the brass candlesticks, one on a chair on each side, and lit them.

I was sorry when it was done, because she was beautiful and she'd been good to me, in bed and out. But she'd got mixed up with the Jerries and she done them blokes to the Gestapo, however you look at it. Or so they said, and they were beyond listening to reason. Like I said, it was her story she told me, and I mayn't have taken it all in. It sounded fair enough, but it was her words against theirs, all the way. I don't even know if they'd've done all what she said, but I think she might have copped a bad time. That weekend we'd come pretty close. I wanted to help her any way I could, because she was mine now. So I suppose it was all right, and anyway what else was I supposed to do?

After a while I finished cleaning the place up. I shaved and dressed and got my gear together. I stood one last time in the bedroom and looked at her lying there. The low sun was striking in and bringing back the shine to her hair where it spread out on the pillow, but her face was white as the sheets. Then I went out and shut the door.

Up the road, it was like a reception committee. Old Wolf-face and the Brat and Big Stupid were there, unshaven and puffy-eyed, hunched up in their old coats, with their armbands and their old Lee Enfield rifles. I think they'd been waiting all night for me to go.

And here was the Yank, all spruce and smooth-shaven, with his uniform pressed and smelling nice, and with a gun on his hip like a cowboy. I could see that the froggies were put out by it, because they could see themselves having to stand outside the door, as it were, like three poor ponces, all over again.

Hi fella, says the Yank, and he offers me a Camel and a light.

Ta very much mate, I says, you can have her now, and good luck to you, I says. And I walks off up the road. I never looked back.

After a few minutes I heard him open the front door – it was a summer morning, remember, and sounds carried. Then I heard him holler out, and then the other three running down the road gabbling at one another.

I went on walking over the hill and I didn't turn round. All the same I'd like to have seen their faces, first his and then theirs, when they bust in and found her lying there in state like a dead empress. Like an imperial whore. Which she was.

Well, that's Saul Scourby's story as I've retold it and stretched it and filled it in and padded it out and no doubt put down more falsehood than truth. I'm finishing it towards midnight on Bastille Day nineteen-seventy-three, whatever that may mean. I've written it out in sadness and in anger, both for the bleak time when it happened and for the squalid age in which we now live. In all the time between, nearly thirty years, this story has haunted me, to the point where I've set it down unwillingly, doubtfully, in spite of myself. I've written without planning and with little revision. Often I've been on the point of chucking the whole thing in the fire, but I haven't. It's been like a tough old ugly cat that won't drown and won't go away. So let it live.

Sometimes it appals me, and sometimes I think it's the finest love-story I know. Cruelty and mercy share the same human heart.

The Second Midnight
Andrew Taylor

'An intriguing story, told in sharp, vivid prose . . . an excellent novel.'
Yorkshire Post

As war looms in Europe, Hugh Kendall is a troubled young boy. But when his hated father offers him the chance to visit Prague, he feels it could be a turning point in their relationship. It quickly becomes a watershed in his life, however, when his father – on a low-level, undercover mission for British Intelligence – is forced to leave Hugh in the hands of the resistance fighters to ensure his own return to England.

Homeless, without a family or a language he can understand, Hugh must discover the laws of survival – in a country riven by war, where invaders and freedom fighters alike are untrustworthy. The only ray of hope is Magda Scholl, daughter of a Wehrmacht colonel, a 'good' Nazi, and even that is overshadowed by the presence of Scholl's fanatical son Heinz. It is Magda's love and Heinz's hatred that will lead Hugh eventually to the ultimate confrontation . . .

'A truly compulsive yarn, unputdownable, and with it Andrew Taylor graduates into the big league.'
The Citizen

FONTANA PAPERBACKS

A Breed of Heroes
Alan Judd

Alan Judd has written a very funny and very disturbing novel about a battalion's four-month tour of duty in Armagh and Belfast during the early 1970s.

Charles Thoroughgood is a young subaltern in the Assault Commandos, Sandhurst-trained like his fellow officers but in his case a graduate too. He and his men have to endure the thankless task of patrolling the streets through weeks of boredom and occasional outbreaks of horror. The tragedies and the madnesses, the personal and military confrontations, that Thoroughgood is involved in or that he ironically observes, are related by Judd with great humour and precision, and with an unusual degree of sympathy. The result is an exceptionally fine first novel full of comic power, awkward army farce and bitter human incident.

'A funny, intelligent and frightening novel.' Victoria Glendinning, *Sunday Times*

FONTANA PAPERBACKS

Bryan Forbes

Also available in Fontana

The Endless Game

'One of the best, most convincing espionage novels I've read in a long time' Martin Cruz Smith

Caroline Oates was little more than a vegetable. KGB torturers had seen to that in Berlin ten years previously when the Austrian network was blown apart. So why kill her? And why now?

Alec Hillsden must find the answers. First, to avenge the brutal, heartless killing of his mistress of years ago. Even more, to uncover the most dangerous player in the endless deadly game they're all involved in – the hate game, the game of espionage.

'Has strangler's grip' *Guardian*

'Totally believable' *Standard*

FONTANA PAPERBACKS

COLD NEW DAWN
Ian St James

'Page-turning potential to pull in the
punters'   John Nicholson, *The Times*

Keir Milford dreams of fame and fortune
as a Fleet Street journalist until he meets
Dawn Wharton, a vivacious young actress.
Hurt by her rejection he pursues a career
in the Army and makes a fortune selling
missiles to NATO . . . and clashes bitterly
with his father.

In a brilliant story which sets father against
son and mother against daughter, *Cold
New Dawn* tells of a family torn apart by
the Arms Race. Fact rubs shoulders with
fiction, revealing bribery, corruption and
scandal in high places . . .

'The fascinated reader cannot put the book
down'
          Des Hickey, *Irish Sunday Independent*

Duncan Kyle

'One of the modern masters of the high adventure story.' *Daily Telegraph*

GREEN RIVER HIGH
BLACK CAMELOT
A CAGE OF ICE
FLIGHT INTO FEAR
TERROR'S CRADLE
A RAFT OF SWORDS
WHITEOUT!
STALKING POINT
THE SEMONOV IMPULSE

FONTANA PAPERBACKS